# JAGUAR'S MATE

## A CRESCENT MOON STORY

Katie Reus

Cover art: Jaycee of Sweet 'N Spicy Designs
Author website: www.katiereus.com

Jaguar's Mate/Katie Reus -- 1st ed.

ISBN-13: 978-1-63556-103-6
ISBN-10: 1-63556-103-5

eISBN-13: 9781635560909

## CHAPTER ONE

Sapphire startled awake at the sound of her cell phone ringing. She'd turned it on low before going to bed after a long shift as manager at the Crescent Moon Bar and Grill.

Her heart rate kicked up a notch when she saw that the number was Luna's, her oldest friend. Their parents had been literal hippies and best friends, hence the Sapphire and Luna monikers.

She swiped her thumb across the screen. "Hey, everything okay?" It was five in the morning and too early for Luna to be calling. Sapphire worked odd hours but her friend didn't.

"Not really." Luna's voice was hesitant. "It's Leslie."

Sapphire swung her legs off the side of the bed. She knew where this was going. And she didn't think she was going to get back to sleep after this. "Did he hurt her again?" she asked, rage filtering through her.

Luna's daughter had mated an abusive wolf about six months ago. The wolf hadn't been like that before though. No, he'd saved his controlling, abusive side until after they'd been officially mated. And from what Luna said, their alpha wasn't stepping in to take care of things. Not that Sapphire was surprised, considering Luna's alpha was a jackass.

Sapphire had offered more than once to drive up to Wyoming and pick up both Luna and her daughter, but Leslie kept telling her mother no, that things were fine. And Sapphire couldn't force them to take her help.

"Yes. I mean no, not tonight or anything. But she let me know that he's going out of town for a work trip. She's got four days alone. She's ready to run but I can't help her get out of here on my own. Because his brothers will be watching her."

Sapphire woke up fully at that. "She told you she's ready to go?"

"Yes. She's done."

"I'll help you out." She strode to her closet and grabbed a sweater from one of the hangers. Tugging it over her head, she said, "Are you being watched?"

"I don't think so. But I *know* she is. He's given her instructions that the only people she's allowed to see are me or a select few female packmates that he approves of." Luna snorted with derision. "I don't know how it's come to this. If I could, I'd take her and leave right now but I know his brothers would try to stop us and then there would be bloodshed. And...Leslie is pregnant. I want to get her out of here so she and the baby can start a new life. I want my baby girl to smile again. Every time I see her she looks defeated. I think getting pregnant is what pushed her to finally stand up for herself."

Sapphire's fist clenched around the hanger she still held, so tightly that it snapped in two. "I'll be heading out within the hour. I've got to talk to some of my pack-mates. My alpha is out of town as well as our second-in-command, but we've got a lot of strong wolves. If they didn't have the jet, I'd fly in, but as it is they're not here. You say he's gone for four days?" Sapphire was going to bring weapons, even if her wolf side didn't care for them. And she couldn't do that on a regular flight. Not to mention her wolf side hated flying anyway. And an edgy wolf on a plane? Not a good idea.

"Yes, but if I was a betting she-wolf, I'd say it's really three days. He's probably messing with her simply because he can."

"All right. Let me get out of here, then. I'll keep you updated on the progress of my trip but expect me there within the next twenty-four hours. I'll be driving straight through."

"Thank you," Luna said softly. "I don't like bringing you into this."

"Stop with that. You should have left that pack a long time ago."

"I know," she said softly, sadly.

Sapphire instantly chastised herself. "Sorry, I'm not judging you."

"I know. Just...get here soon."

"I will."

"Thank you."

Sapphire shoved her cell phone in the pocket of the jeans she'd just pulled on. She needed to talk to Asher in person.

Sapphire hurried out of her condo, not bothering to call or text him first. He and Ella lived a couple floors above her in the pack-owned beachfront, luxury condominium complex in Gulf Shores, Alabama. She felt a little bad because she was likely going to be waking him up, but Ella was currently out of town visiting her sister and he'd had to stay back because both their alpha and second-in-command were out of town. As of right now he was basically in charge of everything.

As she stopped in front of his condo, she thought she smelled something familiar—someone familiar. The sudden wild, sensuous scent of *him*, that male she'd been trying to get out of her head for a month, jarred her senses.

But there was no way Eli was here. Because that would be insane.

She shook off the thought of him. She had a hell of a lot more important stuff to deal with right now. Though she hated bugging Asher, she knocked on his door.

She was surprised when it swung open less than five seconds later and he was fully dressed. His eyes widened slightly. "Everything okay?" he asked, going straight into warrior mode.

"Everything's fine with me. But I have a big problem. And I'm really sorry to bother you so early."

He shook his head. "No worries. A friend of mine got in a couple hours ago."

"Friend?"

"Yeah. He's out for a run."

She nodded once, stepping inside as he moved back. Sapphire was glad it was just the two of them. An outsider didn't need to hear any of this. Quickly she launched into her issue, barely taking a breath as they headed for his kitchen. Thankfully, he immediately went for the full coffeepot and poured her a mug. Her packmates really did know her well.

She barely drew a breath to take a sip of the coffee. Once she was done laying out everything, he was silent for a long moment. Then he said, "I can't go with you. The pack would likely be fine but I've got to be here because Grant and Max are gone."

"Oh, I know. I didn't expect you to come with me. But since you're in charge right now, I know you'll be more aware of who can afford to take the time off than anyone else." And Sapphire knew without a doubt that her packmates would step up to help if they could. It was why she was proud to be part of the Kincaid pack.

Before he could respond, she heard the front door open but ignored it, not really caring that he had company one way or another. Or she thought she didn't care until Eli Scott strode into the kitchen, wearing basketball-style shorts and no shirt.

Her eyes widened at the sight of all that bare skin. His chest and abs were ripped with muscles—and she'd kissed all those ridges and... *Nope.* "What the hell are you doing here!" she blurted, making his eyes go wide even as the scent of surprise rolled off Asher.

"Sapphire, this is my friend Eli. We've been friends for decades and we served together about sixty or so years ago."

Sapphire blinked at the revelation, annoyed at herself that she'd reacted so strongly. She knew Asher had been in different branches of the military over the last century or so, having to change it up on occasion because shifters didn't age the same as humans. It shouldn't surprise her that he was friends with her one-night stand, but it did. Hell, Eli was a two-night stand if she wanted to get technical.

Which she didn't. "Nice to see you again," she muttered before turning back to Asher. She didn't have time to deal with the surprise of him arriving. "Look, I need to be gone within the hour. I told her I'd be there as soon as possible. With the jet gone, it's better for me to drive anyway. I've already started thinking up various scenarios for getting her and her daughter out, but I definitely need backup. Who can I take with me?"

"You have a friend in trouble?" Eli asked, interjecting himself into a conversation that was not his business.

Before she could answer, Asher nodded. "She does. And since you're the best tracker I know, I'd appreciate it if you go with her." Asher completely dismissed her as he looked at his friend and started to explain.

Seriously, what the hell was going on? Was it just a coincidence that he was here? She'd left his very comfortable hotel bed in the middle of the night a month ago—and she hadn't even told him her real name. She'd had an itch that she needed to scratch and he'd been the sexiest male she'd ever met.

As in ever. Holy hotness, the jaguar was all lean, sleek muscle. His dark hair was cut military short, showing off a ridiculously chiseled jawline. Even so, he wasn't classically handsome. He was too rough around the edges, had far too many scars. And his eyes... They were brown, but there was nothing simple about them. The little flecks of amber in them seemed to glow when he was turned on. Even though he looked to be in his thirties, with shifters that was always deceiving since he was pretty close to being a hundred. Maybe even older.

She'd felt a little bad—okay, a lot bad—sneaking out of his room, but she wasn't the settling-down type. And he'd already started to show possessive, protective traits after only spending a couple days together. So she'd done what she always did when uncomfortable with anything relationship-oriented. She ran.

"I'll go," Eli said the moment Asher was done.

"Excuse me? I'm not going anywhere with him." She turned her glare on him. "Why are you even here?"

"Don't flatter yourself if you think it's to see you— *Sally*."

For some reason his words stung even though she was the one who'd snuck out of his place. And she'd given him a fake name. Damn it. She had no moral high ground to stand on right now. "Then why are you here?"

"Catching up with an old friend," Asher smoothly interjected.

She turned back to her packmate. "There's got to be someone else in the pack I can take with me right now. Someone I've worked with and have a good relationship with."

"The packmates I'd normally send are either expecting or their mates are pregnant. We're simply stretched too thin right now."

She gritted her teeth, knowing it was the truth. She been racking her brain, trying to think of who she could take with her that wouldn't be needed, and there wasn't a great choice right now. She did have some limited choices, but... Gah, with his military experience and being a tracker, Eli would be the best shifter to bring. And there was no sense getting all twisted up over it. Right now wasn't about her, but her friends' safety.

"Fine. I've got to pack a small bag." She looked over at Eli, meeting his steely gaze and ignoring the flush of heat and awareness that spread through her. "Can you be ready in ten minutes?"

He simply nodded once.

All right, then. She hurried out of the room, trying to wrap her mind around the fact that Eli was coming with her on a rescue mission. The male she'd never thought she would see again. The male she'd been trying to forget—unsuccessfully.

More unwanted heat spread through her but she squashed it fast and hard. There was no time for that right now.

She had a job to do.

# CHAPTER TWO

"Did that go the way you thought it would?" Asher asked dryly.

Eli scrubbed a hand over his face. He hadn't meant to be rude to her. The truth was, the reason he was in Gulf Shores *was* to see her—because he'd been looking for her. The sneaky little vixen who'd given him the wrong name, the woman he couldn't get out of his head—the female he was almost certain was his intended mate. She'd disappeared from his bed in the middle of the night like a thief and he'd been hunting her ever since.

"I didn't expect any of that," he muttered. He'd been planning to *casually* run into her and hopefully, eventually, start courting her properly. Because according to Asher, she was commitment phobic. Asher also seemed to think there was more to it but had no details for Eli. "Am I really the only shifter you can spare to send with Sapphire? If you've got more packmates, we'll take them with us." Because no matter what, her friend was in danger and he wanted to help.

Asher shook his head. "Seriously man, any other week I would've had a handful of wolves to send. With Grant and Max both out of town and half the pack seemingly pregnant right now, I just can't spare anybody. I would go myself, but—"

"No, I get it. You're in charge right now. You've got responsibilities." Something Eli couldn't relate to. Not on this type of scale anyway.

For so long it had just been him. His friend Asher had been like that once upon a time as well. But now he was mated and part of a pack. And mated to a jaguar, of all things. The thought made Eli smile. The wolf had good taste because jaguars were fucking awesome.

"Anyway, I guess it's a good thing I didn't unpack. I'll be out in a couple minutes." He hurried to the guest bedroom and grabbed a few of his things, dumping them straight back into his pack. Then he took the world's fastest shower. After his long run—an attempt to expel some of his frustration at having been separated from Sapphire for over a month—he needed one. And hell, he wanted to smell good for her. They were about to be trapped in a vehicle for as long as it took to get to Wyoming, and then to wherever they were taking her friends to safety.

After he was done, he found Asher waiting for him with a to-go mug of coffee on the countertop.

"I packed a cooler of food and water for you guys too. You won't need to stop except to rest. Make sure you alternate driving shifts so you get enough sleep. And I want to be updated with what the plan is when you get there."

Eli snorted softly. "Okay, *Dad*."

Laughing, Asher rubbed a hand over the top of his head. "Sorry, I've been in parent mode all week. I swear it's like with our alpha out of town, my packmates have forgotten how to do the simplest shit."

"Or more likely you're just cranky because Ella is gone."

His lifelong friend grinned in the way only mates did when thinking about their other half. "True enough."

Grabbing everything, they headed downstairs and found Sapphire already waiting for him, a duffel bag and a cooler of her own at her feet. She half-smiled when she saw the cooler Asher was carrying.

Jaguars needed to refuel, but wolves could be crazy when it came to food. It was part of their DNA or something. They always had to be snacking.

"We can take my Jeep," Sapphire said, leaning down to pick up her stuff.

His instinct told him to take over, to grab her things for her. And not because she wasn't capable—she-wolves were amazing—but because he had this driving urge to take care of her. But he knew exactly how well that would go over.

Eli shook his head and motioned across the private, gated-off parking lot. "I've got a truck with a camper."

Her gaze followed his and her eyes widened slightly. It was faint but just a hint of pleasure rolled off her, the scent sweet. "Damn. That looks like one of the original Airstreams. It's hard to tell though, because the new ones are 'retro.'"

"The body is from the sixties. I restored the entire interior. Everything is state of the art."

She nodded once, approvingly, and for some reason he felt his chest puffing out like a damn peacock. Jesus, what was wrong with him? "If we need to stop and rest for a couple hours, we can just sleep in there."

"That definitely works better. I'm ready if you are." She met his gaze straight on.

Was he ready to be in an enclosed space with the leggy, blonde she-wolf whose scent drove him completely crazy? Yeah, he was fucking ready.

She nodded once, her expression slightly haughty—and he liked it. Even if she didn't want to be doing this with him, she wasn't afraid of him. He was glad, because that was the last thing he wanted.

Once they got on the road, Eli was quiet as Sapphire started making phone calls. It didn't seem to matter how early in the morning it was, she was calling packmates and letting them know that she'd be gone for an indefinite amount of time. The sound of her voice was soothing as she went over the details of the restaurant and bar she'd managed for years.

Though he didn't belong to a pack or pride, he knew that shifters didn't technically own property. Not usually anyway, though there were exceptions. But normally the pack owned everything, and if someone needed something, it was provided. Even if she didn't own the place, it sounded like it meant a lot to her. And from the limited time they'd spent together before, that was at least one thing she hadn't lied about. So far it seemed the only thing she had lied about was her name. *Sally.* So ridiculous to lie.

She continued making call after call, including to a pack in Montana that was apparently close enough to where her friends lived in Wyoming. That must be where they were going once they'd saved her friends.

"So you have a place we're taking your friends once we get them out of trouble?" he asked as she ended the call.

"Yes. One of my former packmates lives with a pack in Montana now. And I know for a fact that they'll keep my friends safe once they're officially under the new pack's protection and in their territory. And if Leslie's soon-to-be-former mate comes sniffing around looking for trouble, he won't last long." There was a bite of anger to her words.

"How long have you known them?"

"I know Leslie, but I've never been close to her. She's from a younger generation. Luna, however, is one of my oldest, dearest friends. Our parents once spent a year traversing the country in campers with us. We were twelve then. It was one of the best years of my life." There was a note of wistfulness in her voice.

"What happened to Luna's mate?" he asked. It was rare for mates to separate. Usually only in the case of abuse or neglect. And if she was mated, then he would have taken care of this situation—and taken out the wolf abusing their daughter.

"He died when Leslie was two. It's just been the two of them for so long. Luna never wanted to mate again... His death hit her hard and I don't think she ever got over it."

"She loved him, then?"

"Oh yeah. David was perfect for her. Those two..." Sapphire shook her head slightly, a trickle of sadness rolling off her. "He'd never have let this happen. Hell, Leslie's mate would be dead right now if David was alive."

If Eli had been human, that might have sounded odd, but shifters were very different than humans. They didn't have long, drawn out trials when it came to...well, anything.

He nodded. Asher had given him a pretty thorough rundown of what was going on, though Eli was certain there were more details Sapphire could fill him in on later. For now, however, since they had quite a drive ahead of them, he had a few burning questions for her.

He glanced at her. "So, you want to tell me why you ran out on me in the middle of the night? And why you gave me a fake name?"

She blinked and he realized he'd surprised her. "You're not going to make small talk or beat around the bush, huh?"

"I don't see the point in doing that." Not after what they'd shared. Had it just been a fling for her? It had meant way more to him. And at the time it had seemed like it meant more to her too. Then she'd disappeared.

She lifted a shoulder and glanced down at her phone at an incoming text. After replying, she set it on the center console. "Technically it wasn't the middle of the night. It was early in the morning."

He snorted softly. "Smartass."

"Fine. I just didn't want to deal with the hassle of making awkward small talk or whatever in the morning."

"Or whatever?" He snorted again. "That sounds like a lot of bullshit."

"Maybe it is. But that's all you're getting from me now. Look, I had a great time with you. I'm pretty sure we both had a great time. Can we just leave it at what it was and forget it ever happened?"

"There's no way in hell I can forget what we did together. The sounds you make when you come are forever etched into my brain." She was so passionate and wild, he still remembered the feel of her claws pricking into him as she'd come. She'd actually apologized afterward for losing control, but he'd loved the bite of pain because it meant he'd pushed her beyond all control.

She shifted slightly against the seat and he noticed that her cheeks tinged pink as she glanced out the window.

Fine. He wouldn't push her now. But the reason she'd given him for running out was garbage, that much he was sure of. "How about you pick some music for the road, then? And tell me more about Leslie and this asshole mate of hers?"

She let out a soft sigh and reached for the radio station. "I can definitely do that. And because I don't think I've said it yet, thank you for coming with me. I mean, I know Asher asked you to, but seriously, thank you. You have no loyalty to our pack."

"I'm not going because he asked me to. I'm going because *you* need help." He didn't want her to mistake this for anything other than what it was. Though in all honesty, he probably would've helped anyone with a situation like this. But Asher didn't give him orders. No one did.

She shot him a surprised look, then opened that delicious mouth of hers as if she was going to say something. But she quickly snapped it shut and started scrolling through the stations instead.

He tried not to inhale her wild lavender scent too deeply as she settled back against the seat. It was difficult though, because her scent was intoxicating.

Hell, everything about her was. She was probably five feet ten inches, and all long, lean legs. Since he'd seen her completely naked, he knew exactly how toned and sleek she was too. And it was impossible to get the images of her stretched out on his bed out of his head.

They'd met at a grocery store of all places. He hadn't even been looking to hook up and he'd been under the distinct impression she hadn't either.

But one conversation with her and he'd been addicted, desperate to see more of her. Rolling his shoulders once, he took a deep breath as she settled on a station. They had hours together now and he wasn't going to waste a single moment with her.

Whatever reason she had for running, he was going to find out. Then he was going to break down all her walls and convince her to give him a chance. His jaguar was not walking away from this alluring she-wolf.

# CHAPTER THREE

Sapphire settled in across the booth from Eli. They'd been driving for fourteen hours straight and they were both ready for a break. The food in the coolers had been fine, but she'd needed to get out of the truck and stretch her legs. Her wolf did not like being cooped up. She could and would do it for her friend, but she didn't have to like it. Thankfully Eli seemed to think the same thing because he'd jumped at the chance to stop.

"Is it wrong that I want to order the entire left half of the menu?" she asked, only partially joking.

He snorted out a laugh as he shook his head. "I'll order the other half then and we can share."

The place they'd found in the middle of nowhere was an all-day breakfast diner, which was just fine with her. Because breakfast was the best meal of the day. And she could admit she enjoyed spending time with Eli. But she was glad to be out of the truck. Being trapped with him for fourteen hours had wreaked havoc on her hormones.

Their waitress—Darla, according to her name tag— smiled widely as she reached their table, her gaze riveted to Eli. "What'll you have to drink?"

Eli frowned slightly and nodded at Sapphire. "Why don't you take her order first?" His tone was so subdued, slightly different from the jaguar she'd been driving with most of the day.

On the road with him, it had been easy to see why she'd quickly fallen for him a month ago, and then fallen right into his bed. Not that she'd been able to forget why she'd been into him. He'd been stuck in her head for the past thirty-three days. But who was counting? "I'll have a coffee and a water."

Eli ordered his own drink and asked for a few minutes to decide.

"Where should we stop after this?" she asked. "Unless you want to keep driving through the night." They'd both been awake all day. It had been mpossible to sleep when she'd been so wired up. Sapphire was still desperate to get to her friend, but the fatigue was starting to weigh on her. Not to mention fighting her attraction to him was draining.

"I checked my phone and there's a campsite a couple hours north of here. It's right on the way. And we don't need to make a reservation for it. If we stop there for a bit, we'll only have eleven hours left after a short nap. Unless you want to go farther than that?"

"That sounds good. I can do a couple more hours after this. And I need to run. What's the place like? Will we be able to run?" She didn't bother dropping her voice because humans ran all the time. She was also wildly curious what he looked like in jaguar form.

"It's on a lake. We should be fine. It'll be good to stretch my legs," he murmured as the waitress approached the table again.

Sapphire had barely glanced at the menu but breakfast joints were usually the same. So she ordered a plate of bacon, sausage and a giant stack of blueberry pancakes.

Darla's eyes widened slightly but she nodded and wrote it all down. To Sapphire's amusement, Eli ordered even more than her.

She grinned as the waitress took their menus. "We probably look like pigs," she said, laughing. "Or maybe she thinks we're high."

"I'm sure she doesn't care."

"Oh, I'm sure she doesn't care what *you* order. Because I'm pretty sure she wants a slice of you on her plate." Sapphire laughed lightly because the human woman kept stealing glances over at Eli.

Not that she blamed her; he certainly had a presence. While he wasn't classically handsome, he still stood out. Not that she cared. *I don't*, she reminded herself. That human woman could check him out all she wanted.

She rolled her shoulders once, fighting off a growing edginess that had been simmering all day. Being in such close proximity to him for so many hours had her feeling off-kilter in general. But she wasn't going to give in to insanity. It would do no one any good, least of all her. She'd just end up with her heart broken. "So did you ever catch that rogue shifter you were hunting?" she asked quietly, referring to the job he'd been on when they'd met a month ago. He was a tracker who hunted down rogue shifters and returned them to their packs for punishment.

She'd been out of town, just taking a break from her pack, and his scent had drawn her in at first. That wild, sexy scent that made her wolf go crazy.

He nodded once. "Yep. Found him and turned him in to his alpha. I don't think he was long for this world."

She lifted a shoulder, glancing out the window. It was already dark outside and the stars created a beautiful, glittering blanket high in the sky. It was gorgeous this far out in the middle of nowhere. "Well that's what he gets for preying on defenseless humans. Jackass," she muttered.

"You're going to tell me why you ran out on me," he murmured, his voice all sin and seduction.

She snapped her gaze back to him, taken off guard by his ballsiness. "Is that right?"

"That is right. I can be very persuasive." Again with the seduction in his voice as he dropped it another octave.

She forced herself not to shift against her seat even as she fought back her desire for him. She didn't want him to scent it on her. Instead, she narrowed her gaze at him slightly. "That almost sounds like a challenge."

"Maybe it is."

Before she could respond, Darla was at their table, re-filling his coffee that definitely didn't need refilling, and completely ignoring Sapphire's mug.

"That's okay, I didn't need anything," she muttered as the woman walked away.

Eli slid his mug over to her and it warmed something inside her.

"Seriously, I'm fine. I'm not even done with my coffee." But his thoughtfulness definitely counted. And if she wasn't so dang cursed when it came to men, she might take a chance on him. But that wasn't a risk she was willing to take. For the first time in...well, ever, she hated that she couldn't take a chance on Eli.

When her phone buzzed in her back pocket, she pulled it out and scanned the incoming text from Luna. "I think our plan is in effect. Luna mentioned to one of her packmates that an old friend might be coming into town tomorrow, just passing through. That's set the stage for us being there."

"Did your alpha get back to Asher?"

"My alpha actually texted me earlier. He said he'd make the call-in to Luna's alpha as soon as I let him know we were close to the territory."

Shifters weren't supposed to enter other alphas' territories without asking first. Obviously accidents happened but it was shifter protocol to let them know if you were going to be in their territory. Considering Sapphire had been in the area before and was a lifelong friend of Luna's, her arrival wouldn't look out of the ordinary. "I actually think bringing this camper is going to be really good for us. It makes it look like you and I are simply taking a long trip." Which was their cover story. And the camper definitely sold it.

He grinned at her, and that wild wickedness in his expression that made her panties melt was back. "It might also make sense for us to pose as a couple," he murmured.

Oh, how she wished. "No way. We're just two friends taking a road trip together. So get that out of your head right now."

"Oh, it's never far from my mind. I told you, I can't get the sounds you made out of my mind," he said.

*Dammit.* He was definitely messing with her and it was clear he enjoyed it. She sniffed once and looked out the window, trying to ignore him until Darla arrived with their food less than sixty seconds later. The human had a big smile for Eli, which annoyed Sapphire, but at least she had food now.

If she couldn't have Eli, she'd settle for pancakes. She let out a sigh of appreciation as she inhaled the warm scent of her stacks of blueberry pancakes. This was definitely going to make everything better.

Hopefully it would help her to get his words out of her head for a little while.

\* \* \*

"This is gorgeous." Sapphire stretched her arms over her head as she looked out over the moonlit lake glistening in front of her and Eli.

It was fall, and while there were people at their campsite, there was no one down by the lake, which was a plus for them. She'd already checked in with Luna, and thankfully Leslie was staying the night with her mother, saying that she was going to be baking treats with her for the pack. Not that Leslie should have to give a reason to anyone for wanting to stay with her mother, but for now Sapphire knew she was safe. And soon she was going to be a whole lot safer. They both would be.

"It sure is," Eli murmured.

When she looked over at him, he was staring at her with all sorts of heat in his eyes. Not to mention the simmering lust she could scent rolling off him.

*Dang it.* This was not good. Because she was feeling really weak right now where he was concerned, and when it came to Eli she didn't think she had much control. Her wolf had been edgy in the last month since running out on him. And now that she'd been with him for sixteen hours straight, her wolf side was all happy and ready to come out and play.

In more ways than one. Which could not happen again.

She cleared her throat. "I'll probably just head over to the cluster of trees and undress so I can shift."

"I'll come with you. And you can peek at the goods if you want." He gave her one of those feline smiles that only cats could pull off. Dammit, this jaguar was all about getting under her skin. And into her pants.

She nearly groaned at the thought because she was ready to take said pants off for him. *Damn it. No more of this.*

Annoyed with herself, she turned and practically stomped off for the trees as if she was an adolescent. She didn't even look at him as she started stripping. Shifters weren't weird about their nudity and she was no exception. And even if she had been, he'd already seen her. And she'd been raised by hippies.

Still, she took a sort of perverse pleasure when she heard him suck in a breath behind her.

"Like what you see?" she asked without turning around.

He simply made a growling sound.

Which just made her snicker to herself. If he wanted to get under her skin—and clearly he was trying—she was going to get under his too.

Once she'd bundled her clothes, she glanced over her shoulder to find him completely naked, and doing the same thing to his own clothing. He glanced at her, and the heat was definitely there. Only now it was full-blown lust.

The amber specks in his eyes practically glowed with it.

Unable to hold his hot gaze, she turned away and shifted. The quick burst of pain gave way to a kaleidoscope of pleasure as the world before her shimmered and changed. Soon skin became fur and she was on all fours.

Eli nudged her side gently with his nose and she yipped at him, glad to have a partner to go running with. Even if it was with the male who was making her crazy. And holy cats, he was gorgeous. He was a black jaguar with gorgeous amber eyes, and was pure, sleek predator. She could stare at him all day and not get tired.

Turning away from him, she stared at the forest beckoning them. She'd been living at the beach for so long, and while she loved it and her pack, a change of scenery was always nice. Especially scenery like this. The trees rose high into the sky, starting to lose their leaves and giving her a good view of the stars above. The scent from their campfire lingered in the crisp, chilly air, making this the perfect evening to go for a run.

She made a jumping, playful motion at him once and then took off, daring him to race her.

He was so silent she didn't hear him behind her so when he jumped down in front of her from the trees five minutes later, she laughed inside. Jaguars were so playful. Hell, cats were playful in general. She was glad that Eli was no different.

And not so deep down, she wished things were different for her. That she wasn't cursed. Because Eli was wonderful. No doubt he'd make someone a perfect mate.

Another part of her really considered getting naked with him as soon as they got back to the campsite. But that was just inviting trouble. She shoved off those thoughts and sprinted through the woods, her paws quiet against the fallen leaves and dirt.

The two of them ran for an hour straight, looping around the giant lake and back. Even though it was dark, they'd heard a couple people traipsing through the woods, just taking a walk, so they'd avoided them completely, not wanting to scare some random humans.

As they reached their original spot, she rubbed her nose against Eli's side and was pleased when he nuzzled his face against her own. This wasn't sexual, just the way shifters were when they played.

*Double dammit.* He was so adorable and wonderful. Why couldn't things be different?

Once they shifted back to human form, she didn't bother grabbing her clothes. No, she needed a very cold dip in the lake right about now.

"What are you doing?"

She glanced behind her. "Jumping in the lake."

His eyes widened. "It's freezing."

"Thanks, Captain Obvious." She snickered as she made a break for the lake, completely naked. The moon was nearly full tonight and all the illumination they needed. But the stars were twinkling too and everything was brilliantly illuminated. If she'd been in the right frame of mind, it was kind of romantic.

She let out a short yelp as her feet hit the water. But then she just went for it, diving completely under. After the day they'd had she was taking a quick dip to rinse off. Because his camper didn't have a shower and she didn't feel like trying out the facilities right now.

When she came back up, she was surprised to find Eli sitting at the edge of the water, fully clothed. "Not brave enough to come in?" she asked. Both her human and wolf side loved this, loved the water in general. Ocean, lake, it didn't matter.

"Hell no. I always knew wolves were crazy."

She grinned. "You have no idea." It was on the tip of her tongue to say something flirty about him getting naked and joining her but she held back. It was probably a good idea that he was keeping some distance right now. At least one of them was thinking clearly.

Lord knew, she wasn't. Not when it came to the very sexy jaguar right in front of her.

CHAPTER FOUR

Sapphire stretched out on the double bed, her legs
kicked out as she combed through her damp hair.
"You really weren't kidding about decking this place out.
I love the wood floors." He'd done an incredible job on
the interior of the camper. Everything was sleek, with
new appliances, white and gray colors, and grayish wood
floors. There were little splashes of color though, with
turquoise throw pillows on the small couch, and the bed-
ding was a paisley pattern of blues, greens and yellows.
Everything was masculine but comfortable. If he'd done
all this himself, it would have been incredibly time-con-
suming.

"Thanks. I love tracking down rogues, but I don't love
some of the crappy motels I ended up staying in. It's easier to travel with this. It soothes both me and my jaguar
to have some sort of familiarity to come home to at the
end of every day."

"Have you ever thought about settling down?" The
traveling life wasn't for everyone, but she knew that jaguars could be more solitary than wolves.

He nodded as he pulled out a bag of marshmallows
and chocolate bars. He'd told her they were going to
make s'mores. "I have. And I've been asked to join various packs and prides."

"Packs too?"

"Is that surprising?"

"Definitely not. I just know that not all packs are like mine." Her pack was very integrated.

"Times are changing, thankfully."

She was pleased that he'd said that, because some shifters could be really weird about same species only living with same species. It made no sense to her. They were all shifters. Hell, shifters or human, it didn't matter to her. Even vampires. "Oh, have you ever met Rex? He's a vampire. He was a bounty hunter before settling down with my pack." And she figured that a bounty hunter and tracker were kind of the same thing.

"Yes. We've run across each other a few times. He's all right as vampires go," he said dryly.

She laughed lightly and slid off the bed. "So what's the plan? Grab a couple of hours of rest, then head out?" she asked as she started plaiting her hair into two long braids.

"I figured you'd want a couple s'mores. I know how much wolves like to eat dessert. Then we should get at least three hours of sleep before we can hit the road again. Even if your friend's mate comes back early, we've still got plenty of time. And I want to be functioning at full capacity if we do have to take on some of her pack-mates."

Three hours would be plenty for them since they were shifters.

Nodding, she smiled at him. He definitely wasn't wrong about wolves and dessert. Or just food in general. And she was glad that her friends were his priority too. She really could get used to this jaguar.

But of course as soon as she did, as soon as she let him into her heart completely, he'd move on. Because of that stupid curse.

She shook the thought away, forcing herself to enjoy the here and now with him. Though it was getting harder and harder to suppress her desire for him.

\* \* \*

"I can just take the floor," Eli said after they'd packed up everything. He'd gone to take a quick shower in the public showers after they'd eaten s'mores. He'd wanted to try to cool down from being cooped up with Sapphire. He wasn't sure how the hell he was going to sleep, but somehow he would try.

"That's ridiculous. We've literally slept together before. We'll just share the bed. It's small but I don't mind."

She might not mind, but being pressed up against her like that was going to affect his dick. He'd been so damn aroused when she'd jumped in the lake earlier, naked, with that freezing water rolling down her supple skin. Her nipples had been rock-hard, definitely from the water, but damn, the picture she'd painted had been insanely erotic.

And he was pretty certain that the cold water wouldn't have done anything to make his erection go away. Because Sapphire was stunning.

Yep, there was no doubt about it. The funny, sweet female was definitely his intended mate. His jaguar knew that without a doubt. He wasn't even sure how, but he knew on a bone-deep level that there was more than simple chemistry between them. But given what he knew about her, he didn't want to tell her and scare her off. He already knew she was commitment phobic, so he had to play this right. That meant getting her addicted to him first.

"I'll probably just shift to my cat and sleep," he said neutrally.

"Oh, okay." There was a hint of hurt in her voice and he didn't like it.

"You deserve to have the whole bed."

"Okay, thanks." She frowned slightly but slid onto the mattress and curled up on her side.

Feeling like a jerk even though he'd done nothing wrong, he said, "If you really don't mind, I'll join you." *Because this isn't a stupid idea or anything.*

"Okay."

He inwardly berated himself even as he slid into bed with her. Maybe he was secretly a masochist. Because lying next to her would be torture that might kill him. But what a way to go.

She glanced over her shoulder and gave him a soft smile. Her long blonde braids fell down her back and onto the pillow as she settled in. He had the insane urge to pull the little ties out and run his fingers through her hair while she rode him. Or hold on to her braids as he took her from behind. Something they'd done over the two days they'd basically been chained to the hotel bed together.

Flashes of their time together flipped through his brain like images from a camera. Sapphire naked. Her on top of him. Underneath him. Her blonde hair flowing around her breasts as she slowly rode him. Him wrapping his fist around her long hair as he pulled her back against his chest. *Fuck.* What the hell was he thinking?

He wasn't, that was the problem.

Lying on his back, he stared up at the ceiling. He'd turned off all the lights but some moonlight streamed in through the sheer curtains. Maybe if he counted sheep it would help. He nearly snorted aloud at the ludicrous thought.

Ten minutes later, he realized nothing was going to help. Nothing but Sapphire.

Or maybe he could go for another run and tire himself out. Because the last thing he needed was to get no sleep and be off his game later. He wasn't sure what exactly he'd be walking into, but according to Sapphire's friend Luna, Leslie's mate had wolves from their pack keeping an eye on her.

Wolves that wouldn't want to let her leave the territory. And if that wasn't some backwards bullshit, he didn't know what was.

When Sapphire suddenly turned over, clearly wide-awake, he said, "You're awake." *Way to state the obvious, dumbass.*

"We need to sleep. I know that. But I can't seem to turn my brain off."

"We're going to get your friends out of there," he said quietly.

She cleared her throat. "I can't sleep because I keep thinking about *you* and all the time we spent together. About those two days."

He sucked in a breath at her admission. "Tell me the real reason you left," he murmured. He wanted to understand, to know exactly why. Because he needed to know what he was up against. Asher had seemed to think she was against relationships, but didn't know why. Maybe a male had hurt her in the past? His jaguar snarled at the thought, already plotting the pain and suffering of this imaginary male who might have hurt Sapphire.

She opened her mouth once then snapped it shut. "You won't understand."

"How about you tell me, and find out whether I do."

"No. Because I know how crazy it sounds. But it doesn't change the fact that..." She trailed off and rolled onto her back. "I don't want to confuse things between us. But..."

"What?" he pushed.

She turned her head slightly, looking at him again. "Maybe we could have a little fun, exhaust ourselves and get a couple hours of sleep?" Heat simmered in her bright blue eyes.

*Ah, hell.* "I don't want to have sex with you just because we need to sleep."

"Fine, how about you have sex with me because we both know it would be amazing?"

He wanted to. He really, *really* wanted to. "No sex. Not until you tell me why you ran out on me. The real reason." When she started to protest, he grinned wickedly. "But that doesn't mean we can't have some fun." He moved fast in the way that only supernaturals could, and straddled her long, lean body. He slid his fingers under the material of her yoga pants, skimming against her soft skin. "Can I?"

She nodded, breathless. "Yes. Definitely yes."

He grinned again, loving everything about her, especially her enthusiasm. She'd been like that when they'd been together as well. Since they'd been separated, he felt like he was missing part of himself. Which he knew was stupid since they barely knew each other, but that was just the way it was with shifters sometimes. He'd always heard what it was like when you met your mate, but he wasn't sure that he'd actually believed in the intensity of it. Now he did. Because he wasn't walking away from Sapphire.

It didn't take long for him to slide her yoga pants off, and he wasn't surprised that she had on nothing else underneath. She'd been commando when they'd met as well. Something that was insanely hot. A little tuft of fine, blonde hair covered her mound. As he tossed her pants to the floor, she quickly tugged off her shirt.

He really hoped he could show some control and hold off on thrusting deep inside her. He had no problem getting her so addicted to him and desperate for him that she would tell him the truth. Because maybe once they got past that wall she had up, she would finally trust him. And once she trusted him, maybe they could have something real.

"I've missed you," he said quietly.

"I've missed you too," she whispered, almost as if it was a confession.

That was what he needed to hear. Stretched out on the little bed in his camper, with only the moonlight filtering around her, she looked like a goddess. She was even better than his dreams. Hell, before meeting her he never could have imagined a female like this.

He leaned down between her legs, inhaling deeply, her scent wrapping around him like a lover's caress. But before he took exactly what he wanted—and gave her what she deserved—he started kissing a path of featherlike kisses along her tight stomach, over her breasts and neck until he finally captured her mouth.

She wrapped her arms and legs around him, kissing him back with a passion he felt all the way to his soul. Everything about her was wild and sensual. There was no holding back with Sapphire. Not in the bedroom anyway.

He teased his tongue against hers, savoring the sweet taste that was all her—and the chocolate she'd had earlier. Watching her eat that dessert had been an exercise in control. She'd made those little moaning sounds he'd felt all the way to his dick.

In that moment he wished he had more than two hands because he wanted to touch and caress her everywhere. He cupped her breasts, teasing her nipples into rock-hard points until she was arching against him, her legs squeezing around his hips as she silently begged for more.

Next time he would give her a little more foreplay, but for now, he wanted to taste her climax on his tongue.

Though he hated to stop kissing her mouth, he trailed right back down her body, kissing her all over as he made his way back between her legs.

She let her thighs open for him as he leaned forward. "Fuck," he murmured before flicking his tongue along her slick folds. The wild scent that was all her was stronger now, filling the entire camper with pure, unadulterated Sapphire.

She arched her hips into his teasing strokes, impatient as ever.

With his thumb, he began teasing her clit even as he continued stroking her folds with his tongue. Over and over he teased her, savoring the erotic sounds of her gasps and moans of pleasure. And when he slid two fingers inside her slickness, she arched off the bed.

If their past was any indication, he was fairly certain that she was close to coming.

Her inner walls tightened around him and he remembered how tight she'd felt when she'd been wrapped around his cock as he'd thrust into her.

*Control.* He swore he had it. Maybe.

He began moving his fingers in and out of her in a rhythm he knew would drive her crazy. It didn't take long for her to surge into climax, her orgasm rippling through her as she cried out his name.

It was music to his ears.

She came with her entire body, arching off the bed as her orgasm seemed to pour through her in wave after wave.

Eventually she collapsed against the bed, a sated smile on her beautiful lips. He knew she was a wolf, but in that moment she looked like a pleased feline. The proverbial cat that had lapped up the cream.

"You're seriously the most beautiful woman I've ever seen," he breathed. He was harder than he'd ever been, his erection heavy between them. It was taking all his self-control not to pin her to the bed and thrust inside her.

She seemed to not know what to say to that and instead she reached for him. When she shoved at his jogging pants, he didn't stop her as she pushed them down his hips. He definitely didn't have enough control to stop *that.*

He finished kicking them off and as he knelt back on the bed, she was right in front of him on her knees. His cock swelled even more, throbbing with each heartbeat.

Smiling at him, their bodies inches apart, she wrapped her fingers around his cock and began stroking.

"I want you to come all over me," she whispered, making his balls pull up impossibly tight.

*Fuck.* His plan to hold out for a little longer died when she talked like that to him. He crushed his mouth to hers as she continued stroking him, her fingers tight and her rhythm incredible.

Cupping her breasts, he continued stroking her nipples as she stroked him, memorizing everything about her.

This woman completely owned him and likely had no idea.

Over and over she continued until he couldn't take it anymore. And he did exactly as she'd ordered him to—he came all over her stomach. When she actually rubbed it on her skin, he felt as if he could come all over again.

Knowing that his scent would be all over her—that others of their kind would know he'd claimed her—did something to his most primitive side.

Even as she pulled him down to the bed with her, he forced himself not to read too much into it.

"That was incredible," she whispered, brushing her lips over his. This time her kisses were softer, sweeter.

He liked both the wild and sweet parts of his Sapphire. He shouldn't think of her as his, but it was too late to stop it now. Because she was his. She just didn't know it yet.

# CHAPTER FIVE

"Take a deep breath," Eli said.

Sapphire was tense right now and he could sense *and* scent it. She was putting off all sorts of wild emotions that were sharp and bitter.

"I'm just anxious," she said. "I want this done and over with."

Meaning, she wanted her friends safe. "I know. But if any of those wolves watching your friend pick up on your anxiety it will trigger their suspicion. We're just two shifters passing through, seeing an old friend."

She snorted softly. "They're going to smell the sex on us so we might as well be lovers. It makes more sense for a jaguar and wolf to be traveling together if they're intimately involved anyway."

He had no problem pretending to be lovers—and there was no pretending involved at this point. She seemed to be softening to him as well. Sooner or later, he'd tug those walls of hers down.

Nodding, he glanced in the side-view mirror. They were about an hour from their destination and he knew Sapphire could get her emotions under control by then. She just needed a distraction.

Since he didn't know Luna or Leslie this wasn't personal for him, and he was able to relax more than her.

He could be more focused. And though he didn't want to treat her friends like a job, he was going to think of them as one because it would help his objectivity in getting them to safety. In the end, that was all that mattered.

"Tell me about your family," he said.

"I know what you're doing."

"Getting your mind off everything? Yes. I'm not trying to hide that. So come on."

She sighed, but a small smile tugged at her lips. "Fine. My parents are still alive and still doing their own thing. We talk a few times a month when they take a break. They're very nomadic."

"And you're not?"

She lifted a shoulder. "If I get the itch to travel, I go roaming for a while, but my wolf side definitely needs a pack. The two of them? They are each other's pack. They are all they need. Growing up with them was amazing, so while I'm not completely like them in that sense, they're great parents. I got really lucky."

"How often do you see them?"

"Now that they've learned how to FaceTime, I see them fairly often. But if you mean in person, a couple times a year. They plan trips to come see me and I'll go see them as well. But for logistical reasons, they usually come to me because they don't stay in one place for very long."

"How do they survive like that?" Shifters lived a long time and being part of a pack or pride offered a lot of financial stability. He made his money by tracking shift-ers who'd gone rogue, but his was a unique profession.

"My dad is a handyman and my mom makes jewelry." She paused for a moment and then said her mom's name. "Indigo Zappa."

He turned to look at her, lifting an eyebrow. "She's well-known."

Sapphire grinned and nodded. "I know. Trust me, they're not hurting for money. And they have very few needs so they just keep racking up money, letting it ac-cumulate in a bank account they very rarely touch— other than to donate to various shifter causes. I tried to get them to talk to a financial planner but they just brushed me off." She sounded exasperated but it was the kind of exasperation you feel when you truly love some-one.

"My parents are like that too," he said quietly. "As far as having a small pride. Jaguars are different though. Well, compared to wolves. I know there are larger prides all over the world but my parents just had my brother, my sister and me. I'm the youngest. We considered our-selves a pride. When the three of us moved out, my par-ents didn't bother looking for another pride. They're content with just the two of them."

"Are your siblings mated?"

"One of them. My sister is happily mated with three cubs of her own. And my brother...I don't actually know what my brother is doing right now. He's very secretive about his jobs."

"I'm officially intrigued," she said.

Eli realized he'd let out a growling sound when her eyes widened slightly. "I didn't mean I was interested in your brother like that. Holy crap, is this you being jealous?"

"You shouldn't be intrigued by any male other than me." He didn't care if he sounded possessive of her. He was. After last night he was pretty certain he wasn't going to be able to play it cool or pretend he wanted something casual. It wasn't the way he was wired. He wanted Sapphire for more than a night or two. He wanted forever.

She didn't say anything for a long moment, but he could feel the weight of her gaze on him as he continued driving down the highway.

"So...last night was nice," she finally said, the tone of her voice changing slightly. They hadn't actually talked about it since they'd gotten on the road. "Or I guess it was this morning. My sense of time is kind of screwed up right now."

"It *was* nice. More than nice," he tacked on.

"So...once we get my friends to safety, maybe we can take the long way back to my pack?" Her tone was careful, bordering on neutral.

He shot her a quick glance. "What does this mean for you? Is it still casual for you?"

She didn't answer right away. Instead she glanced out the other window. "Look, I'm going to tell you something. And I know it sounds crazy but it's not. So if you laugh at me or make light of it I will punch you in the throat. Not while you're driving because I'm not going to put myself in danger, but it will happen when you are least expecting it."

"I'm not going to laugh at you."

"Fine. You want to know why I'm not into relationships? The first three relationships I had ended with my current lover at the time finding their intended mate right after me. And I'm talking *immediately* after. All of them basically wanted me to fix them. Like they were freaking projects I didn't want to work on. And as soon as they got their shit together, they literally left me and went on to find their mate. I'm freaking cursed! So now I don't do relationships."

He wasn't sure how to respond to that. But he damn sure wasn't going to laugh.

"Well?" she demanded.

"Well what?"

"Aren't you going to say something?"

"You told me not to laugh," he said dryly.

She punched him lightly in the thigh. "I told you you'd think it was dumb."

"No, I don't." He reached across the center console. Something like that happening, three times in a row, was bound to make an impression on her psyche and put her off relationships. Especially if it happened when she was a younger wolf. But those males were stupid, and Eli wasn't. They hadn't seen what they'd had in Sapphire, but he did. "How old were you when this happened?"

"I was younger, in my thirties."

And now she was in her seventies. Well, that explained her commitment-shy tendencies. "Did you love any of these guys?"

"No." The answer was so quick, he believed her.

He'd have been able to scent a lie regardless and he was glad she'd finally told him the truth. This was something he could work with. If some shifter had broken her heart? It might have been harder to push past. But this...curse? Yeah, he could deal with that.

Because it was time to break this so-called curse.

# CHAPTER SIX

Sapphire kept her smile pasted on bright for her friend Luna. They'd met at a local place for brunch. It was one of those cute little mountainside towns with lots of downtown shops. About half were owned by shifters while the other half were human-owned. As far as Sapphire knew, humans didn't know about the existence of shifters here, but they were very friendly with the pack. Well, some of them. Because Sapphire knew for a fact that Leslie's mate was a jackass and not well-liked. But he didn't work in town. Leslie used to...until her mate demanded she stay at home.

And if they had a better alpha—who was also a cousin to said jackass—Leslie would be safe right now. "We definitely need to do mimosas," Luna said, her smile just as bright and easy as Sapphire's. She'd left her dark hair natural and curly around her shoulders today.

Leslie was smiling as well, but there was a certain amount of tension rolling off her.

Which was normal considering her mate was an abusive asshole, but it was also because it was almost time to leave.

*For good.*

They wouldn't be staying the night or dragging out their time here. They were getting her friends out and leaving. Because the longer they stayed, the bigger chance that Leslie's mate returned home early. There was no guarantee he would stay away the four days. As of right now Sapphire couldn't even tell Leslie was pregnant so she must have just found out. Yep, now was the perfect time to get her out. While they still could. Because once her mate found out she was pregnant, he'd never let Leslie out of his sight.

Next to her, Eli was quiet but friendly as he leaned back in the chair at the outdoor table they'd chosen. Leslie had been insistent they sit outside, and though she hadn't said why, Sapphire understood. She'd seen three wolves at a bar and grill across the street who weren't doing a very good job of spying on Leslie and Luna.

According to Luna's text to her earlier, Leslie's mate was angry she was meeting with strangers while he was gone. Even though Sapphire wasn't a stranger at all. But apparently the thought of Leslie meeting a friend who had a male companion was too much for his tiny brain to handle.

Which pretty much guaranteed he was already on his way back home.

"We're also going to have to do a little shopping," Leslie said, her voice surprisingly light. "I know how much you love to shop," she said to Sapphire.

Sapphire had no feelings about shopping one way or another, but this was all part of the plan she'd set up with Luna. They needed to be on the move and get Leslie and

Luna away from their watchers. Just for a little bit. Getting them out of their line of sight was what mattered.

And then the plan that Sapphire and Eli had put into action was officially on.

It was dangerous, but she'd relayed everything to her own alpha and Asher so they were well aware of what she and Eli were doing.

"Yes, definitely. I need to get gifts for my packmates. You know what wolves are like. They've all demanded I bring back food for them," she said, laughing. Though the truth was, once she got her friends to safety, she probably would pick up some gifts for her packmates. All of the food variety.

The rest of brunch went by smoothly, and Sapphire noticed another wolf joined the three across the street. So there were four in total and one seemed to be moving around. Of course there could be more but this lined up well with what Luna had told her.

Once they were done and Eli paid the check—charming jaguar—they all stood. Sapphire linked arms with Leslie, leaving Luna to walk with Eli. Normally she'd be chatting Luna's ear off about something or other, but this wasn't a normal situation. The last thing they needed was Leslie getting close to a strange shifter male and those other wolves getting all crazy and intervening.

Because so far they seemed to be keeping a decent distance away. Sapphire didn't want to tempt fate.

"This shop is my favorite," Leslie said as they strolled down the sidewalk. Her light brown skin seemed paler than normal and Sapphire wondered if it was because her mate had been keeping her indoors more. She couldn't ask now, but she would later. "It's Christmas themed," Leslie continued. "They have everything. Ornaments, decorations, you name it, they probably sell it. It's three stories of awesomeness."

"Sounds good to me," she said as they entered the store. Once the four of them were inside, Sapphire said, "Are you sure about this? There's no turning back once we take this next step." The wolves outside wouldn't be able to hear them, especially not over the Christmas music blasting in the store.

"I'm sure. Do we make the move now? Or later?"

"Now's as good a time as any. We'll stay in here for a while and you guys can go out the back door." Luna had told her that all the stores on this strip exited into a back alley that led to a neighboring street, and that was perfect for what they planned. "Are you sure you want to?" she asked again. There would be no room for error now so Leslie had better be certain she was truly ready to leave town.

"I am. He was threatening my mom," Leslie said. "It's the only reason I didn't try to leave before now. I trust you to get us out of here."

*Oh, hell.* Sapphire hadn't known that. It made sense why Leslie had stayed with him as long as she had though. "Okay, then. Now go before one of them gets the bright idea to check out the back of the stores. They were all across the street when we stepped inside."

Luna gave Sapphire a brief hug before she and her daughter moved through the displays, with Eli and Sapphire following them. But instead of heading out the back like Luna and Leslie, they strode up to the second floor and were greeted by a pretty human woman wearing a Mrs. Claus-inspired outfit.

They both nodded politely, holding hands as they strolled through the displays, looking at the various themed Christmas trees. Leslie hadn't been kidding, the store was kind of amazing.

"Oh, I'm definitely buying you this," Eli said casually as he headed toward one of the windows overlooking the street. He picked up a small jaguar Christmas ornament.

"How many do you see?" she murmured.

"They're all across the street. They didn't split up. I say we've got maybe five minutes before one of them gets nosy and heads inside. Or around back."

"That should be enough time for the girls to get away. At least for this phase of the operation."

"Let's wait until one of the tails gets nosy then start making a purchase. I don't think they'll approach us. They might, but we'll see."

Sapphire didn't think that the wolves would approach them in the middle of town. No, she knew exactly what they'd do. They would wait until Sapphire and Eli left and were alone and then confront them.

It was what Sapphire and Eli were counting on for their plan to work.

So now they were going to shop and stop at a bunch of stores, stalling long enough for Luna and Leslie to get to a safe place.

# CHAPTER SEVEN

"I think this is going to work," Sapphire said, her heart rate slightly jacked up as they headed down the highway. They'd spent an hour in town "shopping" and the wolves following them had been very anxious. Two of them had disappeared for a while, then she'd seen all four of them reconvene near the parking lot where she and Eli had retrieved his truck and camper.

She was fairly certain the only reason the males hadn't approached them was because there had been another family with a camper next to them and the teenagers had been in selfie-taking mode.

"I do too. We've had a tail for about three miles." Eli's voice was smooth and calm. "They'll make their move soon."

Oh yeah, she was preparing for it. Because even if they had a plan, there was no way to predict how these wolves would react to anything. If they reacted poorly, there was going to be a fight. And she had no problem taking on a bunch of jackass wolves. She-wolves were definitely vicious when necessary and she was no exception. Not when it came to protecting her friends.

Eli was an incredibly reassuring presence. Everything about him was in control and calming, making her wolf relax so she was ready for this confrontation.

"Here we go," she murmured as an F-150 pulled in front of them and basically slammed on the brakes.

"Jackass," Eli muttered, even as he slowed his truck.

Sapphire tensed slightly in her seat, all her muscles pulling taut. The stretch of highway was nearly deserted, with barren land spreading out for miles on either side. As they pulled to a stop on the shoulder, both of them got out, furious. She glanced behind them and sure enough another truck was parking behind them. Two wolves were in the front seat.

Two other wolves got out of the truck in front of them.

"What the hell is this?" she shouted, facing down the wolves from the truck in front of them. She immediately recognized one as a wolf who had been tailing Leslie as they shopped and ate today.

"Where the hell are they?" the guy demanded, keeping his focus on her, though he watched Eli warily.

Eli leaned against the front of his own truck, his body language casual, but even Sapphire wasn't fooled. His jaguar was in his eyes, his predator right beneath the surface. Unlike her, he didn't answer to an alpha, so if he took out all of these shifters he wouldn't be hurting a pack or pride. Of course that was a double-edged sword because he didn't have a pack or pride to protect him from retribution.

"What the hell are you talking about?" she said.

"Luna and Leslie. Where are they?"

She frowned as if confused and glanced at Eli. "Back in town, I guess. Why are you doing this? Did something happen to them? Is she hurt?" She was careful to phrase everything as a question. When it came to shifter senses, they could scent lies easily.

"You know damn well where they are." He nodded once behind her and she turned to see the two other wolves stalking toward the camper. One put his hand on the door, as if he was going to open it.

"Hey! That's ours. What the hell do you think you're doing?" She placed her hands on her hips, completely embracing the role of the enraged she-wolf. She could do indignation well when warranted. Not that she had to stretch much to act here. She was pissed.

"That's my camper so you better tread carefully," Eli said, finally speaking for the first time, pushing up off the truck. He was all sharp, clean lines and muscle. The man really was a work of art.

"You're in my alpha's territory." The wolf's smile was smug.

"Technically we left that territory half a mile ago."

The other wolf blinked once.

"You might want to check your property lines a little more carefully. I've got it pulled up on my GPS if you need." Smugness rolled off Eli. That smugness wouldn't stop these wolves from searching the camper if they were determined though.

"Look," Sapphire said, stepping forward. "What do you want? This is ridiculous. If my friends are hurt, I want to know about it."

The wolf opened his mouth to answer, but Eli cut him off sharply. "You're on camera right now." He motioned behind him to the small device hooked up to the dashboard. It was basically a cop cam. "And this feed is being dumped to a server run by her pack. So you really want to tread carefully…unless your alpha wants to go to war over something?"

For the first time, the wolf looked slightly off-balance. He cleared his throat and looked at the other wolf next to him. "We just want to search your camper."

"Why?"

"We can't find Luna and Leslie."

Sapphire blinked, feigning confusion again. "What does that have to do with us?"

"They're hiding in your camper."

"No, they're not." She said it with pure conviction, no scent of a lie rolling off her. No doubt this wolf scented the truth on her too.

He frowned again. "Fine. Let us look inside."

"It's unlocked. Go for it," Eli said.

The wolf, clearly in charge, nodded at the two males standing by the camper. They finally opened the camper door and headed inside. It wasn't large and there was nowhere to hide. Less than two minutes later they stepped outside and shook their heads at the shifter in charge.

He looked frustrated but focused his attention on Sapphire and Eli. "Where the hell are Leslie and Luna?"

"Why the hell would you ask me that? I'm not either of their keepers. In fact, last time I checked, slavery was outlawed." she snapped.

Oh, he did not like that response. But he also had no reason to hold her and Eli as they weren't in his alpha's territory anymore. She wondered how far these wolves would go to get their answers. Because if they attacked first, they would be starting a war.

She pulled out her cell phone and glanced at the incoming text. Inwardly she smiled, though she kept her expression neutral. Leslie and Luna had made it to the meeting spot.

"We're leaving now," Eli said, cutting through the growing silence. "You have no reason to hold us and we've been accommodating for whatever bullshit this is."

Even though he looked pissed, the wolf nodded after a long moment and motioned for the other two wolves to head back to their own truck.

Sapphire was silent as she and Eli got back into the truck. Once they pulled away and had made it about a mile down the road, he said, "Looks as if they've headed back the way they came."

"You think they put a tracker on the camper?" she asked.

"I think it's a very real possibility." She didn't question him when he pulled off of an exit and found the nearest gas station. After doing a thorough scan, he found a small tracker tucked underneath the bed. He grinned when he found it. "We're going to have some fun."

She grinned back, having an idea where he was going with this. "I'm game."

As soon as they dumped the tracker somewhere that would lead the wolves on a wild chase, they'd meet up with her friends and get them to safety.

## CHAPTER EIGHT

"I don't know how to thank you for this," Luna said for the tenth time as they settled on a bench where the Kendrick pack was having a casual get-together.

Sapphire's pack was close with the Kendrick pack after one of their own mated with the second-in-command the year before.

They'd arrived two hours ago and had gotten settled in fairly quickly with the friendly Montana wolf pack. Right now Leslie was surrounded by a bunch of she-wolves and was being nurtured and smothered with love. As it should be.

"You better stop with that," Sapphire murmured to Luna a she watched the wolves talk, eat, and even some dance out in the open clearing where tables of food and drinks had been set up. Pretty much your standard wolf pack life. They liked to eat, drink and be merry.

"I'm serious." Luna reached over and squeezed her forearm once before taking a sip of her wine. "I didn't know he'd been threatening me," she continued. "Leslie only told me after you arrived. I think...she was afraid if something happened and you couldn't make it, that I'd grab her and run anyway."

"It makes sense now that he was threatening you. I...I don't know what happened to your pack."

"Me neither. In the last decade these weak male wolves seem to have infiltrated our pack. It's disgusting. I should have listened to my instinct and left before but I was comfortable and things weren't terrible. Hell, Leslie's mate seemed normal. When I say there were no red flags...there weren't. He blindsided my girl. Me too." Her jaw clenched tight even as her claws started to extend. "I kept begging her to leave with me. I thought she was brainwashed or... Hell, I don't know. I just couldn't understand why she wouldn't leave."

Sapphire wrapped her arm around Luna's shoulders. "You guys are safe now. No one is going to infiltrate Kendrick territory. They've secured their borders even tighter since Erica and Hudson had twins." Erica was a former packmate of Sapphire's who now had adorable twin boys who would soon be one year old.

"I know. I think I just need to talk things out a bit... But now that we can breathe some and I can see Leslie is okay, tell me more about this jaguar whose scent you're drowning in." Luna's voice was pitched low, but it did nothing to hide her amusement.

"We don't have to talk about him." Sapphire's gaze strayed to where Eli was talking with some of the wolves, including Hudson and the alpha, Malcolm. Of all of them, Eli was definitely the sexiest, hands down.

"Come on. He's really into you, if the possessive way he's been watching you all night is any indication. And it's clear you're into him."

"He's...fine. We're fine. We're just...I don't know. Things between us are...nice."

Luna glanced at her and lifted a dark eyebrow. *"Fine* and *nice?* Want me to get you a thesaurus?"

Sapphire gently nudged her best friend. "Shut up. Ugh. I don't know. He wants a commitment, I think. He doesn't want casual, at any rate."

Luna snorted. "And let me guess, you got all stupid—"

"Hey!"

"I'm your best friend, I get to use that word. Like I was saying, I know exactly what happened. And I swear if you bring up that curse, I'll lose it."

Sapphire shot her a frown. "I *am* cur—"

"Don't say it. Do not say the word. You are not cursed."

Before she could respond, Erica strode up, smiling widely at them. "I'm so glad you've joined our pack," she said to Luna, pulling her into a hug.

Sapphire stood as well and hugged Erica. She'd been one of the younger members of the Kincaid pack when she'd lived in Gulf Shores. Now she was a mother and Sapphire could tell how much she'd grown into herself. Her friend had a confidence that hadn't been there a couple years ago.

"Where are the boys?" Sapphire asked, hoping to get to play with the pups tonight.

"Getting into trouble." Erica's voice was dry as she shook her head. "They've been running around all night shifting from human to wolf. I've completely lost track of them and their clothes. I don't even know why I bother dressing them."

"When they turn about four they'll start keeping up with their own clothes," Luna said. "My Leslie was the worst about running around naked, I swear. All the pups in our pack were."

"They definitely keep me busy. So how long are you going to be in town?" she asked Sapphire.

"Ah…a day or so. I want to make sure they get settled in."

"Thank you." Luna smiled softly.

"Good," Erica said. "It's good to see you even if the situation isn't the best. Plus I want all the Kincaid pack gossip, including everything about that sexy jaguar you're hooking up with."

"Yeah, we're not talking about my love life, nosy wolf."

"I beg to differ. I'll get it out of you. Why don't you and Luna come to the salon tomorrow and I'll take care of you. You can fill me in on everything then."

"Ah…" Luna glanced over at Leslie, who was still talking to some of the younger she-wolves, two of whom were pregnant.

"I've already made her promise to come in too. You can make a girls' day of it. After everything you've been through, take this break and pamper yourself. You guys deserve it."

"We're in," Sapphire said before Luna could respond.

"Good, then. Now if you'll excuse me, I need to find my boys before they set something on fire."

"One rambunctious pup was hard enough," Luna murmured as Erica walked away.

"No kidding." Sapphire had always wanted kids, but she'd never let herself think too much about them. She'd always assumed they weren't for her. Because of the thing that she wasn't going to think of.

After spending more time with Eli and getting to know him—and falling hard for him—she was starting to wonder if maybe... *Nope.* Not going down that road. Not tonight anyway.

She was going to do the wolf thing and eat, drink and be merry. For her sanity.

\* \* \*

Sapphire reached for the last piece of triple chocolate cake at the same time that Malcolm, the alpha did.

"I'm just messing with you," he said and scooted the dessert plate over to her.

"Thanks. You almost lost a hand." She kept her expression neutral as she dug a fork into the layers of heavenly goodness.

He blinked once and then grinned. "Noted. It's really brave what you guys did to get your friends here."

She lifted a shoulder. "That's what friends do for each other. And Eli had my back."

Nodding, Malcolm glanced around, looking over the clusters of his packmates scattered everywhere. "Yeah, I like him. Not sure where he went off to though."

Sapphire scanned the crowd of wolves, also wondering where he'd gone. An irrational, jealous side she hadn't realized she possessed was annoyed that she didn't see him. She wanted to know exactly where he was because a few females had disappeared earlier too. Not that she thought he'd run off and hooked up with someone tonight but that weirdly possessive part of her brain was flaring to life.

She did not like this feeling.

"How long are you guys staying?" Malcolm asked.

She'd just started to respond when Eli appeared out of nowhere, like a ghost from the shadows of the trees, and slid an arm around her waist. Holding her tightly, he kissed the top of her head. "We'll be here for a couple days," he answered politely enough. There was a strange edge to his voice.

She glanced up at him, wondering what was going on with him. It wasn't as if Malcolm had been flirting with her or anything, even if he was single. Not even close. He was doing his duty as the alpha, and being friendly to the newcomers. Newcomers that he'd allowed onto his property when he hadn't had to.

Malcolm actually grinned though, and stepped back. "You're welcome to stay as long as you want. We've got a cabin available for you two if you decide not to stay in your camper. Hudson can show you where it is." Then he was gone, being hailed down by one of his pack.

"What was that? I thought you liked him," she said, turning into Eli's embrace.

"I do like him. But I don't like him talking to you."

She blinked. "Wait...you don't like *him* specifically talking to me, or is this a general thing where you don't like any males talking to me?" Because she recognized that predatory look in his gaze now. He was definitely jealous. When he simply lifted a shoulder, she laughed and laid her cheek against his chest, inhaling the wild scent of him. "Is it weird that I like that?"

His body stiffened slightly so she pulled back to look up at him.

"Do you want to get away from the party?" he asked, heat sparking in his eyes. "Or do you need to be here for your friends?"

"They're fine without me. They're assimilating very quickly into this pack."

"Good. We need to be naked, like now."

Warmth spread through her like wildfire at his words. Being naked with him sounded perfect. "Are you finally going to give up the goods for me?" she asked, not joking at all.

He let out a loud laugh that wrapped around her, warming her from the inside out. He looked years younger when he laughed and the sound itself was absolutely intoxicating.

"That's not exactly an answer," she murmured.

He tugged on her hand. "Then come with me and find out."

They got directions to the cabin, though she barely remembered the walk there. All she could focus on was Eli's intoxicating, wild scent as she fantasized about finally getting naked with him again. As soon as they opened the door and stepped inside, Eli had her back flat against the front door as it shut behind them. She wasn't sure if he locked it or not and didn't really care. If someone decided to come in, they were in for a show.

"You're not cursed," he rasped out as he bit her bottom lip, nipping gently.

She had no response for that. Instead she basically shoved his pants off, surprised she didn't rip the button on them.

Before he'd stepped out of them, he was tugging at her shirt. He tossed it behind them as he buried his face in her neck. "And I'm not letting you walk away," he murmured, his voice wicked and sensual as he scraped his teeth along the column of her neck.

Pinpoints of pleasure flowed everywhere as heat flooded between her thighs. Why the hell was he talking? She wanted to feel his cock inside her right now. She'd been missing him for over a month. This was no time to talk. Not when they needed to be naked and doing stuff.

"So whatever you think about your stupid curse, it's not real," he continued, taking off her bra now. "Or if it is, I'm going to break it."

"Shut up and get naked." She grabbed at his own shirt and tugged it off.

He made quick work of the rest of her clothes and had her flat against the door again. Oh yeah, it was time for the good stuff.

She wrapped her legs around his waist as he looked deep into her eyes. "Did you hear everything I said?"

"I heard you. I don't know why you're still talking. You should be fucking me." She wasn't going to touch on anything he'd said. Not right now. She'd just allowed herself to think that maybe things between them could be different, that she wouldn't lose him once she let him into her heart—but she wasn't going to say it out loud.

He grinned and rolled his hips against her. His erection was heavy between them and she loved the feel of it. But she would love it even more if he was inside her.

"Life with you is never going to be dull," he murmured.

"Eli—"

He cut her off with a demanding kiss, his tongue invading her mouth and making her weak in the knees. Breathing hard, he pulled back. "Don't say anything right now. Just be with me. And accept what I'm offering you. I don't want to walk away from you, from us. I feel it on a bone-deep level that you're my mate." He looked shockingly vulnerable in that moment and she understood why. That was a huge declaration to make.

He thought she was his mate.

It was everything she'd wanted to hear. Hell, needed to hear. Because she'd felt the tug too, but she'd been ignoring it because of her own fears. What if she admitted that she thought the same thing and turned out to be wrong? What if she put the thought out into the universe and then he found someone else? His true mate, like all the others had?

But he was nothing like all the others... Oh God, she needed to say something.

"I can see you getting lost in your head right now," he murmured. "You don't need to respond. But now you know how I feel."

"I care about you, Eli. A lot." She tried to force more words out, but her throat seized up. She felt like a coward for not being able to put herself out there like he had, but he covered her mouth once again, taking control.

"Don't think right now. Just feel." This time his kisses were long and slow, his tongue teasing against hers. There were things she wanted to tell him, but right now she just wanted to enjoy the sensation of his body against hers, of the skin-to-skin contact she'd been craving from him.

Reaching between their bodies, she started stroking him even as he ran his hands all over her, teasing and caressing her everywhere.

Her breasts rubbed against his chest, her already sensitized nipples rubbing against him, sending little waves of pleasure to the pulse between her thighs. She'd been without his touch for far too long and felt raw and needy.

When he cupped her mound, testing her slickness, she just about combusted. And when he thrust inside her, she clenched around him, moaning out his name.

In that moment, everything boiled down to just the two of them as he thrust inside her over and over, his thickness filling her. She'd missed him, but she wasn't sure she'd realized how much until that very moment. Being with him like this was almost surreal, like she was coming home in a way she'd never known she needed. She loved her life and her pack, but being with him filled something different inside her. A deeper need, hunger.

She clutched onto his ass, digging her fingers in tight as he drove inside her.

It didn't take long for both of them to climax. Once he reached between their bodies and started teasing her clit, she surged into orgasm at the same time he did.

Pleasure punched through her in sharp, intense waves until they both collapsed against the door. Her arms and legs were loose as she laid her head against his shoulder.

"Now that round one's over, let's start round two in the shower," she murmured. Then maybe for round three they'd make it to the bed. She didn't care where though.

He lifted her into his arms, carrying her through the small cabin with the fierce determination of a shifter carrying his mate.

It was on the tip of her tongue to tell him she saw a future with him—that she wanted one. But something held her back.

Thankfully he wasn't pushing her for more right now. Instead, he turned on the shower to steaming and she found herself flat against the tile this time as he devoured her mouth with his.

Claiming the rest of her fearful heart along with her body.

## CHAPTER NINE

Sapphire smiled at Leslie, who was approaching her and Eli's guest cabin. Eli was off running and she was enjoying her morning cup of coffee. "Hey," she said from where she sat on the bench on the front porch.

Leslie smiled back, carrying a mug of what smelled like chamomile tea. Someone had braided her dark hair into little rows and twisted them into a bun at her nape. Her dark eyes weren't sad, for the first time in ages. "I'm glad you decided to stay a little bit longer. I know my mom loves having you around."

"I love getting to spend time with her. Even when the circumstances aren't the greatest."

Leslie hovered at the bottom of the porch stairs, her expression uncertain. "Look, I just wanted to thank you again—"

"Seriously. You and your mom need to stop thanking me." Sapphire patted the bench seat next to her.

Leslie walked up a few steps onto the porch and sat down. "Well I'm going to keep thanking you anyway. You and Eli put yourselves in danger for me. In more ways than one."

"I know."

"Are you sure that you do?" she asked. "Because I didn't think about the repercussions for anyone but me until we got here."

"If you mean, do I know that I made myself a target? Of course I do. I'm an old shifter. Well, maybe not old compared to some of these guys but I'm old enough. I know your mate will likely try to have words with me or even come after me one day. If he lives that long." She lifted a shoulder.

Leslie blinked in clear surprise. "That doesn't bother you?"

"He won't be the first enemy I've made over the years and he certainly won't be the last. But I don't think he's long for this world. If I had to wager, I'd say he's going to try to come after you here on Kendrick territory—and one of the warriors is going to take him out." Sapphire wasn't sure if she should be so blunt, but she was a she-wolf. And from what she knew about Leslie's mate, he wasn't letting her go. So even if coming after her was monumentally stupid, he'd make a play for her.

Leslie shoved out a breath. "Is it terrible that I kind of already know that? And I feel like a fool for not seeing him for who he was."

"Well, you're not omniscient. You can't keep beating yourself up for this. You are the victim here. You did nothing wrong."

"I could've told my mom earlier that he was threatening her."

"If you had, you two would probably be dead right now. Because Luna would have grabbed you right then and tried to run. And he's got too many wolves backing him up. No, you did the right thing in a literal no-win situation. He's at fault. Not you. And so are your former alpha and packmates who stood by and did nothing." Even thinking about that crappy pack made Sapphire want to set stuff on fire.

Leslie was silent for a long moment, staring out at the cluster of other cabins and forest beyond. "I know you're right. I just hate that I'm in this situation. I always thought that once I got mated it would be for life. He fed me every line possible and I ate it up with a spoon. I never felt that pull that you hear about. The mating pull. But I was attracted to him and thought the mating pull was garbage. Something made-up, for romantics. I was such an idiot." There was far too much recrimination in Leslie's voice.

Sapphire wrapped an arm around her shoulders. "You're not an idiot. And I know you're going to beat yourself up for a while for this because you're just like your mom, but I'm going to reiterate that you did nothing wrong. You got out when you could. You made the smart choices. You're still alive and you're here."

"And pregnant," she whispered, laying her head on Sapphire's shoulder. "I know he'll never let me go because of that reason alone."

Sapphire kissed the top of her head once. "I think things will work themselves out. You just focus on taking care of yourself and settling into your new life here."

"I don't even want to leave the territory. And that makes me feel like such a coward."

"You're not a coward. You feel safe for the first time in a while. And you're keeping yourself and your baby safe. You're being smart. So you should stay here for the near future at least. You just escaped an abusive situation."

"Thank you," she whispered, her voice thick with tears. "Damn it, I'm crying all over you."

"That's okay." Sapphire hugged her tighter, wishing she could take away all of her pain. But nothing would do that. Just time. And closure, if Leslie ever got it.

Sapphire had the urge to hunt down Leslie's mate and take care of him herself but that wasn't her job. She was going to let nature run its course. Because from what Luna had told her, Leslie's ex-mate was kind of a dumbass and would get himself killed in no time at all. Humans might think her thought process savage, but she wasn't human. She was a shifter. And they lived by their own set of rules. Which yes, probably were savage. But there was a reason they had very few domestic abuse issues. Shifters, on the whole, didn't put up with shit like that.

There were very clear exceptions. Leslie's mate and pack included. But they were unfortunately the exception to the rule.

And once word spread of how her pack had betrayed her, had let her mate abuse her, it wouldn't matter if her old packmates begged for their lives. Anyone complicit in the abuse would be hunted down eventually.

That was just the way shifters were.

\* \* \*

Eli shifted from jaguar to human, his black fur and claws receding until he was crouched on the cold ground by the giant oak tree where he'd left his clothing. But...his clothing wasn't there.

"Over here, cat." The sound of Luna's voice made him turn toward the edge of a small pond where she sat, his clothing still in a neat little bundle next to her. She kept her eyes averted from him. "Come change and sit with me."

Though surprised by her presence here, he picked up his clothes and hurriedly dressed. "Everything okay?"

"Yes." The pretty she-wolf with light brown skin and dark eyes stared out over the still, sparkling water. The sun peeked over the horizon now, painting the sky a swath of riotous purples and pinks.

Unsure what to say, if anything, he leaned back on his elbows and just watched the scene in front of him. This place was beautiful so it was easy enough to relax, to simply enjoy the nature surrounding them.

"Sapphire can be prickly," Luna finally said, her tone as mild as before.

"I know."

"She's not likely to change."

"I know. I like her the way she is." And he didn't want her to change. He loved everything about her, even if he hadn't said the actual words. Mainly because he wasn't certain she was ready yet. Though his instinct told him that he was close to breaking down her walls completely.

Luna shot him a sideways glance. "You sure about that?"

"Of course I am. I thought you were her best friend."

"I am. I love her deeply. She's the sister I never had. Sapphire is my family and she's perfect the way she is. Those pathetic males she was with in the past couldn't handle a female like her. I just want to make sure that you can."

His jaguar's annoyance eased back some, the claws he'd felt pricking his palms sliding back in. "I'm not walking away from her. Unless she tells me to leave. And...maybe not even then." This time he would fight for her, tooth and nail.

Luna finally gave him a real smile and nodded once. "Good. You two fit well together."

Yeah, he thought so too.

"How do you feel about pups?" she asked abruptly.

"Ah..."

Laughing, she jumped to her feet with the ease of a supernatural. "I'm just messing with you. Well, just about the pups. If you ever hurt Sapphire intentionally,

I'll gut you," she said, a pleasant smile on her face as she held out a friendly hand to him.

Though he didn't need it, he took her outstretched hand and stood. "I'll never hurt her...and I'll keep your words in mind." Freaking she-wolves could be terrifying on the best of days.

Now he was ready to go find his she-wolf and claim her for good.

# CHAPTER TEN

*Two days later*

"I'll miss them, but it feels good to be on the road," Sapphire said as she and Eli headed down the highway.

"Yeah," he murmured noncommittally.

They'd been driving for a few hours, and each minute that passed she wanted to ask him what was going on inside his head.

For the last couple days they'd been naked half the time. He'd been insatiable—and so had she. But ever since they'd gotten on the road, he'd been a little distant.

And she knew it was her fault. "I'm not good at this," she blurted.

He glanced over at her, frowned. "What?"

"Whatever this is," she said, motioning between them. "Deep down I still think I'm cursed. But I'm also willing to concede that I want to take a chance on us. I just don't know how to have a relationship. Like...will you stay with me when you're visiting? Or will we try the long-distance thing? Or...I don't know. I don't know how to do any of this."

Oh God, why hadn't he said anything? And why did she sound borderline whiny?

Beads of sweat trickled down her spine despite the fact that the heat wasn't on. She definitely wasn't good at this kind of stuff. "What are you doing?" she asked when he started to pull off at the nearest exit.

"We're doing this while I'm not driving. So I can kiss you properly." He glanced at her, his dark, amber-flecked eyes sparking with desire.

Kissing sounded promising, so why wasn't she any less stressed out? She was quiet as he pulled into the parking lot of an abandoned gas station. This whole stretch was pretty deserted except the decrepit old building. But at least there was no one around.

As soon as he was parked he turned toward her, taking her hands in his. "What do you want from me?"

"Everything." It was as simple as that, she realized. She wanted all of him, all the time. But she knew he had a nomadic profession and she...could totally deal with that.

"What does that mean?"

Okay, that was fair that he wanted her to spell it out. "I'm not saying right this instant but my wolf recognizes you as my mate. *I* recognize you." The pull she felt was intense and raw and she couldn't deny it.

Pleasure was clear in his gaze even as he watched her carefully. "My job—"

"I'll travel with you." If she was doing this thing, she was all in. Sapphire wasn't one to half-ass something, and especially not where the man she loved was concerned.

He blinked, a grin spreading across his handsome face. "I was going to say my job is something we can work around. I'm not doing long-distance with you. I want to see your face when I wake up every morning. And I want to bury my face between your legs on most of those mornings."

She laughed even as heat flooded between her thighs. "I love your dirty mouth."

He grinned even wider, leaning forward to brush his lips over hers for a brief moment before pulling back. "Can you really take off time to travel around for a while?"

"Yeah. I already talked to my alpha. It'll be a pain for my packmates but I've covered for all of them at one time or another. Let's take a month and enjoy each other—with no outside distractions." She knew everything she needed to know about him, but she wanted more time with just the two of them. Her wolf was feeling very territorial and wanted Eli all to herself for a while. She wanted him good and claimed by the time he met all her packmates.

This possessiveness was new, but she embraced it.

"Okay, good. There's a campsite not far from here. I know it's kind of early, but we can make camp and relax. And do other things."

"Other things?"

Grinning, he simply started the engine and pulled out of the parking lot. Other things sounded perfect to her. She was ready to have fun with her future mate.

And she was certain that he was hers.

Almost two hours later, they made it to the campsite located right on a huge lake. Sapphire didn't think she would be spending any time in the lake this time, however. She planned on staying curled up in Eli's arms more often than not.

"Luna's texted me a few times," she murmured as they settled in their chairs in front of the fire they'd built. Little wisps of steam from her breath curled in front of her as she read the incoming messages. "Apparently her ex's alpha has reached out to Malcolm and is trying to play this off as a simple misunderstanding."

Eli snorted. "How'd that go over?"

"Malcolm told the alpha that if he wanted to talk about this 'misunderstanding' in person he was welcome to come onto Kendrick territory. Alone."

"What'd that piece of shit wolf say?"

"He never responded." No surprise. An alpha who wouldn't protect his own pack wasn't brave. "How are those s'mores coming along anyway?" she asked, nodding at the two marshmallows he was holding over the fire on sticks.

"Patience, my she-wolf."

"Oh, you'll learn that... Wait a minute. How did Leslie's alpha even know where she's staying?" she asked as ice chilled her veins. Both Leslie and Luna had dumped their old phones and got new ones a couple days ago. Maybe there had been another tracker in the camper? It was the only thing she could think of.

Eli stilled in that moment, and in the silence she scented something that didn't belong.

Wolves. Half a dozen maybe. Nearby too.

"We run, hide, then take them out one by one," he whispered, standing with her even as he scanned the lake and surrounding area.

It got dark here earlier in the day now and they would have to use that to their advantage.

*Pop. Pop. Pop.*

Sapphire jumped into action as bullets pinged into the side of Eli's truck. Reaching for Eli's hand at the same time he reached for hers, they raced for the tree line.

*Pop. Pop.* Dust flew up behind them as they sprinted across the dirt and grass.

She called on her wolf before they breached the tree line, letting the change take over sharp and fast. Her clothes shredded, falling off her as her paws slammed into the ground. Another cluster of dirt and grass flew into the air from a bad shot.

Freaking wolves using weapons? These really were weak shifters. She raced alongside Eli in silence as their pursuers shouted out something behind them. She heard two distinctive male voices but she'd scented more than two.

As they raced deeper into the trees, Sapphire slowed and nudged Eli once before looking up.

He shook his head. She looked up again and growled low in her throat. She wasn't being a martyr. She needed him to take to the trees so he could attack from above.

He nodded and broke off from her, jumping to a nearby lower hanging branch. Damn, he was quiet.

She jumped over a gnarled, twisted root and sank a few inches into a huge pile of fallen leaves. When she saw the tree the leaves had fallen under, she knew what she was going to do. If she'd been in human form, she would have smiled.

Moving quickly and quietly, she backed up into a sort of cutaway in the tree. It was dying, that much was clear. But it would stand tall until a bad storm took it out.

She burrowed down in the leaves, using them to camouflage both her scent and body. In wolf form, she was brown and gray and would blend well enough.

She didn't hear anyone or anything other than some agitated squirrels chirping away at the invasion to this part of the forest. The wolves must have shifted to their beast form. So they'd be quieter, deadlier now.

Hunkered down, Sapphire remained in place, waiting. Watching.

She knew Eli had to be close. There were too many scents in the forest to pinpoint him, but she knew he wouldn't have gone too far from her. That wasn't his way.

Without a doubt, she knew Eli would never abandon her. He would be here to the bitter end, no matter what happened today.

That realization, that shocking knowledge, made her want to kick her own ass for dragging her feet where he was concerned. She'd been afraid of getting hurt so she'd tried to push him out because of her own baggage. And she'd almost lost the man she loved.

That wasn't going to happen today. She was an older wolf, powerful in her own right and not afraid to take on these fools. These monsters who'd helped keep her friends trapped, hurt. She had no fear right now, not for herself anyway. Just rage.

She tensed when a gray and white wolf trotted by the tree, sniffing the air cautiously. Her heart rate increased, but he didn't see her.

She waited.

Another wolf walked by slowly, this one slightly smaller. He was brown and red and when one of his paws landed inches from her front paw, she readied to attack. But he continued on, his nose raised in the air.

Still she waited.

There were at least four. Hell, five, because no way would Leslie's ex-mate let this go. He'd be here too with the males he'd had watching her. So five. Maybe more.

It had been a while since she'd been in a fight, but she was okay with these odds. Especially since Eli was a tracker and renowned for his skills.

From his position Eli would have a bird's-eye view, better than her. So going against her wolf's instinct to attack, she remained where she was, waiting for him to make the first move. Once he did, she'd jump into action.

When a third wolf stealthily slid by her hiding spot, Eli pounced from a nearby tree, landing on the back of the shifter in a wicked-fast move.

That was the signal. Using all the strength of her legs, she jumped up from her position, attacking the closest one with a vicious snarl. She opened her jaws wide before she snapped down on the wolf's neck.

Claws from another attacker dug into her side as she killed the first wolf.

Kicking out, she rolled to the forest floor, tossing her attacker off. Her fighter's instinct had set in, her animal taking over almost completely.

Out of the corner of her eye, she was aware of Eli battling two wolves as well. Knowing he was fighting for his life, she fought for her own. Fought for a chance at a future with him. One that hopefully included many years together.

A new surge of rage pummeled through her as she turned fully on her attacker, not bothering to circle him or play games. She swiped out with her claws, slashing across the face, hard and deep.

He yelped in pain even as she jumped on his back, opening her jaws wide and taking him out with one swift, killing blow. Male wolves might be tough, but she-wolves were just as vicious.

As she tossed him to the ground, another wolf raced out of the forest, heading straight for Eli.

*Hell no.*

Eli flung the wolf he'd just killed to the side like a ragdoll before turning to face the newcomer.

Before she had a chance to make a move, he attacked, every inch the lethal predator.

He moved so fast she barely saw him even with her supernatural vision. He had the wolf pinned underneath him in a second, finishing him off quickly and mercifully.

Which was more than any of these males deserved after virtually keeping Leslie prisoner, and then attacking them here.

Inhaling deeply, she looked around even as she scented the air. It was hard to detect anyone else over the scent of all the blood.

As Eli stepped toward her, the bodies started shifting back to human. Yep, the wolves were definitely dead now.

Which left them with a whole other problem. Disposing of bodies.

At the sound of a soft rustling against the leaves, they both tensed, ready for another attack until two familiar wolves in human form stepped into the small clearing.

She recognized the wolves from Malcolm's pack.

The one on the left lifted his hands up in a gesture that meant they were there in peace as the other one let out a low whistle and looked at the carnage. The one on the left spoke. "Malcolm sent us to tail you guys just in case things went sideways. We'll help you guys get rid of...this," he murmured, looking around.

"We need to take pictures of the faces before we dispose of them. The she-wolf will want to identify her ex-mate if he's here," the other said.

Since they couldn't talk in animal form Sapphire shifted back to human form, just as Eli did.

Then he did a very male, very mated thing and stood in front of her, blocking her nakedness even though nudity was totally a shifter thing.

That was when she realized he was bleeding pretty badly on his side and shoulder. She reached out, trailing a hand down his non-bloody shoulder and arm, touching him gently. Before she could ask if he was okay, he said, "We can help you get rid of the bodies. I don't think there are any more but we need to do a perimeter check.

"There aren't any more. We saw these guys arrive and then disperse. By the time we saw them it was too late to warn you—you'd both already shifted. I'm sorry we didn't get here in time to help you fight them. We'll get rid of their vehicle as well."

"Eli, you're bleeding," Sapphire murmured, trying to keep her fear at bay. He was a shifter and would heal quickly, but she didn't like the scent of his blood, didn't like that he was injured at all. Her wolf was clawing at her, demanding she make things right.

He completely ignored her. "Before we do anything else, we're going to shift, head back and grab some clothes."

She wanted to make sure he was truly okay, but she'd been around male wolves her entire life. He might be a jaguar, but in her experience all males acted the same in certain situations, and all shifters healed fast. She wasn't sure if he was just being macho or wanted to get shit done, so was ignoring her concern, but that strange new part of her desperately wanted to make sure that he was okay.

For now, she shifted with him and raced back to the campsite.

As soon as they made it back to the campsite and shifted back to human form, she scanned him from head to foot. Before she could say a word, he frowned, trailing his hand down her hips. You're bleeding," he said, anger clear in his gaze and tone.

"So are you! You okay?"

"This is just a scratch."

"So is this." Her side would be healed within the hour.

In that moment the weight of her emotions and feelings for him crashed in on her like a tidal wave. She threw her arms around him, holding him close, uncaring about the twinge of pain in her side. Just for a moment, she needed to know that he was okay. That they were going to be okay.

He didn't seem to care about his own wound because he held her tight in return, his strong arms enveloping her.

They had a lot to deal with and she knew they wouldn't be headed on their road trip anytime soon. They'd be headed back to Kendrick territory for now. She wanted to be there when they told Leslie and Luna that Leslie's mate was dead.

But for this stolen moment, it was just her and Eli as they held each other in front of his bullet-riddled truck and camper.

There was no other place in the world she wanted to be.

## CHAPTER ELEVEN

*One month later*

"You sure you're ready for this?" Sapphire asked as they pulled into the parking lot of the Crescent Moon Bar and Grill. After a month of traveling they'd decided to head back to Gulf Shores.

"Yep." Eli was so relaxed about being officially accepted into her pack, as if it wasn't a big deal. But it was for her.

The last month had been incredible—and Leslie was finally free of her dead ex-mate. And Sapphire had heard through the grapevine that Leslie's former pack was no more. The pack had either dispersed or its members been taken out. And Sapphire wasn't losing a bit of sleep over that fact. They'd also discovered a very hidden tracker placed in one of the rear lights of the camper. It had blended well with the wiring, which was why they had missed it. The best they could gather was that Leslie's ex had tracked them to the Kendrick pack via the tracker and then followed the tracker to the campsite. Maybe he'd thought Leslie was there too, or maybe he'd wanted Sapphire and Eli dead because they'd helped her. Didn't matter now.

Eli was out of the driver's side and had moved around to the passenger side before she'd even unstrapped.

"Why are you so relaxed?"

"Is there a reason I shouldn't be?" As she stepped out, he wrapped his arm around her shoulders and held her close.

"No, I guess not. But...aren't you excited?" And that was the crux of her worry. He'd agreed to come back here, to see how living with her pack was after a month on the road, but part of her worried that he'd resent her. That he wouldn't like this static life when he was so used to constant travel.

Frowning, Eli stopped on the gravel parking lot and tugged her until she faced him. "What's going on?"

"I'm worried this life will be boring for you." *Ugh.* Saying her fears out loud felt like she was giving them life.

He blinked, clearly surprised by her admission. "I could never be bored with you."

"Not me, I mean...not traveling constantly."

"I loved my job but I was fucking lonely, Sapphire. I hope we get to travel some because I do enjoy it, but I love you. I know your pack matters to you, and knowing that you'd give it up to travel with me is enough. We're older shifters. Who says we'll be doing this a decade from now? I don't care if we're traveling or if we stay put. I just want to be with you every single day. I've spent a lifetime without you, and now that I have you I'm not letting you go. I promise that doing this isn't a sacrifice for me."

Her throat tightened as tears welled up. "How do you always say the perfect thing?" she sniffled.

"Because I'm perfect," he deadpanned.

That got the tears to dry up. Laughing, she buried her face in his chest for a moment, inhaling his scent, letting it invade and comfort her. "You're certainly not lacking in ego. But that's part of why I love you." This wonderful, sometimes maddening jaguar who'd stolen her heart.

He tightened his grip around her. "We better get inside now or I'm tossing you over my shoulder and we're headed back to our place."

*Our place.* Those two words punched her right in the heart. "Okay, let's do this." They'd settled in earlier in the morning and her alpha had insisted they come down to the bar and grill for a party.

It wasn't as if wolves needed an excuse to party but this was a great reason as far as she was concerned.

When they stepped inside the crowded bar, she grinned when she saw a huge sign stretched up over the main bar top that read: *Welcome home, Sapphire and Eli!*

They were immediately surrounded by packmates, including Ella, who high-fived Eli and told him that jaguars would soon outnumber wolves if she had any say about it.

An hour later, Sapphire looked at the new shot glass in her hand. Talia, Grant's mate—and Sapphire's former coworker—had given it to her. "Why am I doing shots again?"

"Because commitment scaredy-cat Sapphire is now mated, that's why!" Talia tossed her head back and did a shot herself, clearly unwinding tonight. Her inky black hair was pulled up into a ponytail and little stars glittered all over her head.

"Scaredy-cat?"

Talia shrugged. "Scaredy-wolf sounds weird."

Sapphire rolled her eyes but took the shot anyway. As a shifter she had a much higher metabolism than humans, but her packmates had been plying her with a crazy amount of shots over the last hour.

"We've missed you," she continued.

"I've missed you guys too."

"Yeah, right! You stink of sex. Did you two even travel or did you just hole up somewhere and go at it like bunnies?"

Sapphire snorted but didn't answer. They might have traveled, but there had been a whole lot of sex involved. A lot. And she still craved him. Automatically, she scanned the crowd for Eli and found him talking to Grant, Max and Asher. Probably about his new job helping out with security at the casino and hotel.

As if he sensed her gaze on him, those dark eyes with the intoxicating amber flecks found hers. He grinned widely and she found herself grinning right back. She wasn't sure how she'd landed the sexy feline, but she was damn glad she had.

Looked like that stupid curse had been all in her head. Luna had never been so happy to be right and had said, "I told you so" far too many times in the last month.

"Did you hear anything I said?"

Sapphire looked over to find Talia watching her intently. "What?"

"Oh, you are so smitten."

"Well, yeah."

"I'm glad. You deserve it." Talia threw her arms around her and squeezed tight. "Of all the packmates, I always hoped you'd find your other half," she whispered.

Oh hell, now she was going to cry for real. Before that could happen, Eli was suddenly there, wrapping his own arms around her after Talia had stepped back.

Then everyone else faded away. The music pumping over the speakers disappeared and all she saw was Eli. Her jaguar. Her mate.

"I think an hour is good. We've put in our time," he murmured.

"It's our party. We can't leave." There wasn't much conviction in her voice.

"No one will notice if we're gone." His eyes went all heated and sensual and she knew they'd be leaving in less than thirty seconds.

"I don't know," she hedged, knowing he'd take the bait.

Laughing, he tossed her over his shoulder and smacked her butt once. As she expected, a chorus of shouts went up from their packmates as they hurried from the bar.

She had a feeling they weren't even going to make it back to their place before they got naked. She smacked his butt once and a rush of heat flooded through her when he growled again.

Oh yeah, they definitely weren't making it home just yet.

—THE END—

Thank you for reading Jaguar's Mate I really hope you enjoyed it. If you don't want to miss any future releases, please feel free to join my newsletter. Find the signup link on my website: https://www.katiereus.com

Also, flip the page if you'd like to read some excerpts from the Crescent Moon series!

# Wolf's Mate excerpt
## Copyright © 2018 Katie Reus

Erica laid her head against Hudson's chest as she trailed her fingers up his rock-hard abs—and over his plethora of tattoos. Everything about him was muscular and defined, which was common among shifters, wolf or otherwise. But the tattoos? He was the first shifter she'd met who had so many. Most of them were linked to his original Scottish clan or pack related things. Luckily none of them were for any past lovers. Something she would never be okay with.

She knew her time with him was coming to an end, and though she wanted to stall even longer, she shouldn't. Not if she wanted to keep her heart in one piece. Mostly. Because it was cracking already at the thought of leaving him. Of leaving Montana.

"Keep touching me like that and I'm going to be inside you in another ten seconds," he murmured, his voice all rough and raspy, sending shivers down her spine.

The man just had to open that sexy mouth and she was mush. "You say that like it's a bad thing." The truth was it didn't matter if she was touching him, he couldn't seem to keep his hands off her. Something she very much appreciated. Because she liked orgasms. A lot.

"Stay another couple days," he murmured.

It was on the tip of her tongue to say yes. She desperately wanted to. One month with him wasn't enough.

But he hadn't offered her anything. He'd simply asked her 'to stay in Montana'. And while he might not be alpha of the Kendrick pack, he was second-in-command and terribly alpha in nature. Shifters like him went for what they wanted. If he wanted to claim her, for her to stay permanently, he would have asked for that. Simple as that. Because the male was over two hundred years old. He was being honest, she could give him that. He'd never promised her anything and she'd taken exactly what he'd been offering—a lot of fun.

So she might want him—and genuinely want more than just sex—but she wasn't going to throw herself at him. Hell no. She was going to walk away with her pride intact and head back to her own pack. Even if it carved her up inside to do so. Because sometime during the last month she'd fallen for him. Hard. It would have been impossible not to. He'd opened up about his past, brought her breakfast in bed—woke her up with oral sex almost every other morning—and was simply the sweetest man she'd ever met.

"We've been over this." She gently nipped at his bare chest. Damn she was going to miss him. For more reasons than the hard body underneath her.

"You're not on a schedule." He was dangerously close to pouting, which under any other circumstance, would have made her giggle.

But she didn't feel like laughing now. Not when the ache in her chest had settled in deep and wasn't letting up anytime soon.

She pushed up on the bed to look into those startling blue eyes. His dark hair was a little longer than most of his packmates, curling around his ears. "I might not be on a hard schedule, but I still need to get back. It's been a year. My pack needs me." After college she'd started working at one of the pack's salons. Then when the owner had up and mated—and moved—Erica had decided to reevaluate her own life.

So she'd taken a year to herself and roamed around the globe, mainly sticking to the United States. During the last month of her trip, she'd been traveling across Montana and had met the very sexy Hudson Kendrick. She'd never imagined meeting someone like him on her trip. All sexy, surly and incredibly giving in the bedroom—soooo giving. And everything about him was real and honest. What you saw with Hudson, you got.

In response, he simply growled at her, but there was no heat behind it. Not that it mattered, her wolf side knew on an intrinsic level that he would never actually hurt her so even his most terrifying growl didn't scare her. He started to say something when his phone buzzed.

Cursing, he snatched it off the bedside table and then cursed again when he looked at the screen. "It's my brother, we're having another issue on the border. I've got to take care of this."

Though she hated to do so, she rolled off him and let him get up. It was hard not to admire the view as he picked up his discarded jeans from the floor and tugged them on, covering all of that sexy bronze skin.

"I'm probably just going to head out while you're gone," she said carefully, watching him for his reaction.

He froze for a moment before turning to glare at her. "At least wait until I can take you to the airport."

She wanted to say yes but gave a noncommittal grunt. His brother, the alpha, had offered to fly her back to her home in Alabama on his private jet anytime she wanted. Apparently, there was a pilot currently on standby. Which was really nice, but also bad because she'd kept extending her stay for the last week. Because Hudson kept pushing for 'one more day'. Erica knew that if she waited for him to take her to the airport, she'd give him another day, and then another.

And then that whole pride thing? Yeah, she wasn't so sure she'd walk away with it intact. She'd do something stupid and then getting over him would be even harder. Try, impossible.

When Hudson's phone buzzed again, he did that sexy growling thing as he looked at it. More colorful curses followed before he tugged a long-sleeved T-shirt over his head. She stayed in bed, just watching him move, all lethal efficiency. Once he was dressed, with his boots on, he stalked toward the bed and leaned over her, placing both hands on either side of her head, effectively caging her in. Then he crushed his mouth to hers, a possessive claiming she felt all the way to her core.

Unfortunately, he didn't seem to want to claim her in reality. Because sex wasn't enough to keep her here. She wanted more than that. Something she hadn't realized until she'd met Hudson. The sex was great—better than great—but she needed more.

"I'll see you soon. Be naked when I get back."

Oh no, not responding to that. Nope. Because she wouldn't be here when he got back.

Once he was gone, she gave it five minutes before packing up her small bag and trying to ignore the spreading ache in her chest. She had to do this now. She hadn't brought much with her on her trip, because it was a whole lot easier to travel light. Now she was grateful for that. The sharpest sense of melancholy filtered through her as she hefted her bag and backpack up. It was time to go home.

So why did it feel like she was making the biggest mistake of her life by leaving? And why did it feel like she was leaving home instead?

## Falling For His Mate excerpt
## Copyright © 2017 Katie Reus

You sure you know what you're doing?" Sybil asked as they cruised down the main strip of Orange Beach, Alabama.

Andrew just grunted. Mainly because hell no, he wasn't sure. But he was second-in-command of the O'Shea pack. He had to appear to be sure, all the time. Normally he never second guessed himself. He'd also never fallen for a she-wolf before. Yeah he'd had shifter lovers, but Charlie... he'd fallen hard for her. Then he'd screwed up.

"I'll take that grunt as a big fat no. And that you're a dumbass."

He jerked in surprise and glanced at her in the passenger seat. Tall, with long curly auburn hair, she was definitely one of the beauties of his pack. Not that she did anything for him—and vice versa. They were more like siblings. "Dumbass?"

Sybil lifted a shoulder.

"Okay fine. Maybe I am."

"There's no maybe about it. And let me tell you something, even if you get her to forgive you, you're going to have to get her wolf on your side too. If you'd ghosted on *me* like that? Dude, my wolf would claw up your face on sight. On principle."

"I know." He was a wolf shifter too, so of course he knew. They weren't like humans. Their dual nature was part of their DNA, who they were. So the reminder that the female he'd fallen hard for might attack when she saw him? Yeah, not fucking needed.

"It's gorgeous down here," Sybil said a few minutes later.

"Yeah." Orange Beach in early May was definitely that. It was pushing noon, the sky was blue with a few streaks of white scattered overhead. Not that he cared. All he wanted was to get to Charlie. "This is it," he said, slowing as they reached the turnoff to the Kincaid pack 'compound'. His heart rate increased a fraction. Soon he'd see Charlie again.

For the next few weeks, or however long it took all the alphas in the southeast region to meet and discuss potential alliances and what to do about the rash of rogue vampires that had been infiltrating their territories, this was his and Sybil's home. Each alpha had traded a couple of their packmates with other packs.

It was difficult for any alpha to leave their territory unprotected, so they'd come up with this trade of sorts. The logic was that no one was going to attack another pack because if they did, the packmates they'd traded would be killed. Only a shitty alpha would put his own people in danger. And the packs meeting all had strong, honorable alphas. This was just a failsafe to keep everyone in line. Andrew had volunteered, which was strange for a second-in-command to do, but his alpha had let him. Even though it had put their young pack at a disadvantage. He'd needed to see Charlie in person, to apologize. To make things right.

"Pretty sure I'm going to be down here visiting again," Sybil said as he steered into the now opening gated entrance. "I wish we lived closer to the beach." There was a wistful note in her voice.

The Kincaid pack had beachfront property and every member of the pack had an ocean view. According to what he'd learned, each condo was the same size—except the second's, who lived in the penthouse. The alpha had his own home right next door to the condominium complex.

As soon as he'd parked and they'd stepped out of the vehicle, Andrew felt multiple sets of eyes on them. He might only be in his thirties, which was young compared to a lot of the pack members here, but he was still alpha in nature. As second-in-command, he had extra honed senses.

Before they'd taken two steps, Max McCray appeared from the bottom floor of the complex. With icy blue eyes that promised death if he stepped out of line, the male was no one to be messed with. Neither was he. Andrew might be in another pack's territory, but he couldn't be anything other than who he was. And he was not submissive, in any sense of the word.

Striding forward, Andrew nodded and held out a hand to the male who was over a hundred years old. His scent reminded Andrew of the beach in winter. Nothing like Charlie's scent—which was wild blueberries and peaches. Nope. He locked that thought up because if he started down that road, he'd get a hard-on. And that was just embarrassing. He'd been in control of his body since he was a pup. Ever since meeting Charlie, however, his entire world was off its axis.

Something he'd sworn would never happen. He'd seen the way his father was completely whipped by a female, the complete imbalance of their relationship. That was never going to be him. Or that had been the plan.

But here he was. In Orange Beach because he couldn't stay away from a dark-haired female with eyes the color of melted chocolate and a scent so wild and free it unleashed all of his primal instincts. Instincts he hadn't known he even had. As a wolf he was more in touch with his primitive side than his human side on the best of days, but she'd brought out something untamed inside him.

"How was the drive?" Max asked, looking between the two of them.

"Good." Uneventful, which was all he could ask for. He quickly glanced around, taking in the high wall. From the main road he hadn't been sure, but now he could see that the high wall surrounded the entire place, giving the pack complete privacy. And not totally out of the ordinary in gated communities.

"This place is gorgeous," Sybil added. "And I heard your pack has a private pool."

Max half-smiled at her. "Yeah. Lauren's off today, waiting to show you around. Threatened an important part of my anatomy if she wasn't off when you got into town."

Andrew snorted as Sybil laughed. Lauren was Max's jaguar-mate and Sybil had become friends with her the last time Lauren had visited with their own alpha's mate—who was also friends with Charlie.

"Good. She promised me a beach day."

"You guys have a lot of bags?" Max asked as Andrew opened the hatch to the SUV.

"Nah." Andrew hauled out Sybil's overpacked suitcase and his own small duffel bag. What the hell she had in here, he couldn't imagine.

"I'll show you to your rooms. I've got you in separate guest condos. I didn't have any next door to each other, but if you want—"

"We're good with whatever you've given us. And thank you for the hospitality. We also want to offer to help out wherever is needed. I know you're out two packmates right now." Well, four technically, since the alpha and his mate were also away at the treaty meetings.

Max simply nodded as they reached the stairs.

Andrew was glad they were taking them instead of the elevator. His wolf needed to stretch and expend energy. He hoped for a run tonight on the beach, but needed to check with Max about that first. His own pack had enough private property that they could run free whenever they wanted. But this was a different territory with different rules. And a very different terrain.

It didn't take long to reach the fourth floor and when they passed one of the condos, he scented wild blueberries and peaches and nearly stumbled.

Charlie.

The scent was old enough that he knew she wasn't nearby, but it still lingered in the air, the smell more potent than anything else in the long hallway. This was her floor.

And since the hallway was completely glassed in, instead of wide open, it would contain scents longer. He swallowed hard, willing his body under control. Her scent shouldn't affect him so strongly, but his wolf had gone over a month without seeing her, touching her, smelling her... Hell. They'd never even gotten naked together.

Not that he hadn't thought about it—and fantasized about her every night while he used his fist to take the edge off.

A few moments later Max opened a door only four doors down from Charlie's place. The male motioned that he could go inside. He also said some other stuff, but Andrew couldn't focus on his words because all his wolf could think about was hunting down Charlie, marking her, claiming her.

He rolled his shoulders once and dropped his bag in the kitchen as Max said, "You'll be on security at one of the hotels or at Crescent Moon Bar—unless you'd like to help out at the salon instead." He said the last part almost jokingly.

Which told Andrew that Max didn't know about what had happened between him and Charlie. Because she owned the salon. He cleared his throat. "Salon's fine with me."

Max straightened slightly. "You sure?"

Out of the corner of his eye, Andrew saw Sybil fighting a smile. "Yeah."

"We're a progressive pack," Sybil added, not bothering to hide her smile now.

Max glanced between the two of them, shrugged. "Fine. I'll let Charlie know you'll be helping out tomorrow. She's the owner and in charge there. So whatever she wants you to do, you do."

The thought of Charlie telling him what to do, ordering him around should have rankled him. He was too alpha for that. But... it oddly didn't. Even if she clawed him up, he just wanted to see her. Hold her.

"I can just call her myself," he said neutrally. "I'm sure you've got a lot on your plate with your alpha gone."

Max nodded absently as he glanced at his phone. It had buzzed half a dozen times since he'd met them in the parking lot. "Yeah, okay. I'll text you her number. Sybil, I'm going to show you to your place, then I've got a few fires to put out."

Andrew didn't tell the other second that he already had Charlie's number. No, he just waited until Sybil and

Max were gone before he allowed his canines and claws to spring free.

Fuck, fuck, fuck. His body was his to control. Always. But right now, knowing Charlie was so close, his wolf was agitated and beyond listening to reason.

Somehow he managed to force his claws to retract long enough so he could strip out of his clothes. Then he let his wolf take over completely.

Fur replaced skin and for a few moments he was the most vulnerable he'd ever be. It was always like that during a shift. Pleasure and pain mixed together as his primal side took completely over.

Panting, he trotted around the condo, sniffing everything as his beast calmed down. Letting the shift take over was the only thing guaranteed to help him relax.

And he needed to be calm when he went to see Charlie. Because no way in hell was he texting her, giving her a warning that he was on his way. If he did, she was likely to be gone when he got there. Or maybe not because she was the kind of she-wolf to face things head on. She'd more likely just punch him. Either way he sure wasn't waiting until tomorrow to head to her new salon.

No, he'd be dropping by this afternoon. Because he had to see her. To apologize to her. And hope that he could convince her to give him a second chance. The thought of giving up his role as second, the pack that he loved... it was hard. But he couldn't stay away from Charlie anymore. She was his to claim.

*Red Stone Security Series*
No One to Trust
Danger Next Door
Fatal Deception
Miami, Mistletoe & Murder
His to Protect
Breaking Her Rules
Protecting His Witness
Sinful Seduction
Under His Protection
Deadly Fallout
Sworn to Protect
Secret Obsession
Love Thy Enemy
Dangerous Protector
Lethal Game

*Redemption Harbor Series*
Resurrection
Savage Rising
Dangerous Witness
Innocent Target
Hunting Danger
Covert Games
Chasing Vengeance

# SAVANNAH'S COMPLETE BOOKLIST

*Miami Scorcher Series*
Unleashed Temptation
Worth the Risk
Power Unleashed
Dangerous Craving
Desire Unleashed

*Crescent Moon Series*
Taming the Alpha
Claiming His Mate
Tempting His Mate
Saving His Mate
To Catch His Mate
Falling For His Mate
Wolf's Mate
Jaguar's Mate

*Futuristic Romance*
Heated Mating
Claiming Her Warriors
Claimed by the Warrior

*Contemporary Erotic Romance*
Dangerous Deception
Everything to Lose
Adrianna's Cowboy
Tempting Alibi
Tempting Target
Tempting Trouble

# ABOUT THE AUTHOR

Katie Reus is the *New York Times* and *USA Today* bestselling author of the Red Stone Security series, the Darkness series and the Redemption Harbor series. She fell in love with romance at a young age thanks to books she pilfered from her mom's stash. Years later she loves reading romance almost as much as she loves writing it.

However, she didn't always know she wanted to be a writer. After changing majors many times, she finally graduated summa cum laude with a degree in psychology. Not long after that she discovered a new love. Writing. She now spends her days writing dark paranormal romance and sexy romantic suspense.